DONE AND DUSTED

Book 2

Damaged Series

USA Today Bestselling Author

SUSAN HORSNELL

Contents

DONE AND DUSTED

Written by Susan Horsnell

Edited by Redline Editing

Line Edit by Robyn Corcoran

Proofread by Leanne Rogers

Disclaimer

This book is a work of fiction. Any resemblance to persons, living or dead, is purely coincidental. The characters are productions of the author's imagination and are used fictitiously. Real name places are used throughout this book but, events occurring in these locales are purely fictitious and for the benefit of the story only.

Warning:

This book contains sexual content and language suitable only for those 18+

"Sometimes when you're broken, you just need the right people to piece you back together."
Callie

Chapter One

CALLIE

The Past

At thirteen years old, I was alone. I had no-one and nothing.

My mama was a part-time bartender at the *Grey Turtle* bar in a seedy part of downtown Foster near where we lived. Home was a dingy one-bedroom apartment with next to no furniture, no heating, peeling paintwork, and black mold spreading over the walls and ceilings. Mama preferred her drug fix to food and somewhere decent to live.

Three months ago, while working the bar, she was caught in the crossfire of a shootout between two gangs... She died instantly. It was three days later when I found out. I was making a stale-bread sandwich when a knock came at the door. I answered to be confronted by a Child Protective Services Officer who told me about mama and took me away.

Why didn't I know before then, you ask? It wasn't unusual for mama to take off with a couple of druggies from the area and return several days later.

Most days I took myself off to school, no one ever questioned my scruffy appearance since most of the kids from where I lived were the same.

So, off I went with a lady called, Giselle. She took me to her office and I sat quietly while she made a phone call.

"Petra, it's Giselle. I have a thirteen-year-old girl needing urgent placement."

Giselle paused and listened to someone on the other end of the phone before speaking again.

"It shouldn't be for any longer than three months."

She paused and listened again.

"Thanks. I'll bring her by tonight."

She hung up the phone and turned to me.

"I'm going to take you to a home where you'll be looked after while we search for your father. Do you know his name?"

"Nope. Mama said he was a stranger passing through town and all he wanted was her pussy in exchange for some drugs."

"Did your mother use drugs often?"

"All the time."

"Who took care of you, bought your clothes, cooked?"

"I took care of myself and cooked. Clothes came from the Goodwill bin."

Giselle sighed and patted my hand. "Mr. and Mrs. Rostenkowski will be paid money by the Government to feed and clothe you so, you won't have to worry about that anymore."

"I'm not worried, I've looked after me and mama for as long as I can remember."

"Well, now you get to be a young girl. Did you attend school?"

"Yes. Foster City."

Giselle frowned. She obviously knew how rough the area was. "Are your grades good?"

"I think so and my teacher said my brain will get me out of the slums. I like school and my grades are better than the other kids."

She nodded, and I saw the look in her eyes which said, *that's one thing you have going for you*. Heaven knew, I didn't have anything else.

I was delivered into misery that very same evening.

****

"Callie, get your skinny ass down here now." Mrs. R, as she allowed me to call her, bellowed and I wondered what I'd done now.

I raced down the stairs and found her in the kitchen cleaning up Joel, her biological two-year-old. He was covered in white powdery goop.

"I told you to keep an eye on him while I brought the laundry inside."

She hadn't, but after three months in this house, I'd learned you didn't argue. "I'm sorry, would you like me to take him upstairs and bath him?"

She thrust one of his little arms toward me. "Yes, get him cleaned up before his father comes home and sees what you've let him do."

I scooped the little boy into my arms and hurried away. He was a sweet little fella and the light in the darkness of my existence. I closed the bathroom door after we entered, and after turning on the water and ensuring it wasn't too hot, I stripped him of his white covered clothing.

"Fun, Cawee."

I couldn't help but laugh. "I can see you had fun."

Once he was undressed, I swept him into my arms and lowered him into the bath. He kicked his chubby legs, clapped his hands and chuckled when I threw in his plastic duck and a boat.

"I have to wash your hair, you have sticky goop stuck in it."

He gave me a look of sheer panic. "Noooo, Cawee. No wash hair."

"Sorry, bud, I can't leave it like that. If you're a good boy, I'll read you a story when we're done."

"Okay."

Washing the little boy's hair was uneventful, the thought of it scared him more than the actual doing. In no time at all, he was scrubbed clean and dressed in fresh clothes.

"Let's go and read a story while we wait for your mama to make supper."

Joel clasped my hand and I walked him downstairs to the living room. I'd no sooner sat down and the doorbell rang.

"Callie, get that." I swear half the neighborhood could hear Mrs. R when she yelled.

"Okay," I called back.

Joel followed me into the hallway and I opened the door to Giselle.

"Hi, Giselle. Do you want to see Mrs. R?"

"Yes, I need to talk with her. Is she here?"

"In the kitchen."

"Go back to what you were doing, I'll speak with you shortly."

I closed the door and while Giselle headed to the kitchen, I returned to the living room with Joel. He selected a book from a basket which held some of his toys and toddled toward me.

His chubby arms straightened and he held it in front of me. "Storwee, Cawee."

I lifted him onto my lap and opened the book. Joel pointed at the picture. "Owl."

"That's right."

"Callie, can you come to the kitchen please?" Giselle stood in the doorway.

I placed Joel on the floor and encouraged him to play with his toys. Before I'd left the room, he was pulling favorite cars and trucks from the depths of the basket. I followed Giselle to the kitchen where Mrs. R stood. She wasn't happy.

"Am I in trouble?" I couldn't think of anything I could have done wrong.

Giselle placed her hand on my arm. "Of course not, honey. I'm here to tell you, your pre-adoption has been formalized and your new parents are waiting at my office."

I wasn't sure what to think of this news. I wanted to jump for joy at the thought of leaving this place. I wouldn't miss the shouting or the chores I was expected to do. I was more like an unpaid maid than a foster child. There was never enough to eat and I often went to bed hungry. The clothes I was given were only just above the garments I'd had from Goodwill. On the other hand, I would be sad to leave Joel.

"Don't worry about packing anything unless you have something special. Mr. and Mrs. McKenzie have purchased everything you need."

"We can leave as soon as you say goodbye and thank Mrs. Rostenkowski."

I turned toward Mrs. R. "Thank you for having me. Please say goodbye to Mr. R for me."

She nodded sternly, no doubt wondering when she would receive her next slave. I didn't bother to hug the woman, she wouldn't know affection if it jumped up and bit her on the ass.

"I'll just go and say goodbye to Joel." My voice was thick and tears sprang free as I trudged to the living room. I knelt down near the sweet little boy. "Joel, I have to go away."

He turned to me and smiled. "Cawee, pway?"

I drew him into my arms and kissed his chubby cheeks. "No, sweetheart. I have to go to a new home now. You be a good boy for your mama." I kissed him again, stood, and rushed to the front door. Giselle was waiting for me and placed an arm around my shoulders.

"Everything will be better for you with the McKenzie's. They have wanted a child for so long, but because of their ages, they were only allowed a teenager. You'll be good for each other."

I nodded as I sucked back a sob and followed her down the steps to her car. I climbed into the passenger seat and fastened the belt before Giselle turned the key and started the engine. We remained silent as she weaved through the streets back to her office.

****

A beautiful lady stood when we entered Giselle's office. She was tall with long, wavy brown hair and gorgeous blue eyes. When she smiled at me, I knew I was going to like her.

"You must be Callie." She offered her hand.

I gave it a tentative shake. "Yes, pleased to meet you." And, I was.

"My name is Rebecca McKenzie but I would like for you to call me mother."

I frowned, it was a bit soon for me to be calling a stranger, mother. But, I decided it was no skin off my nose. "Okay, mother."

A man stood beside her. He was the epitome of tall, dark and handsome. He stepped forward and offered me his hand. "I'm Patrick

McKenzie. You can call me daddy or Mac. I'll leave it up to you."

I shook hands and lowered my eyes, I felt shy. "Mac, I think, please."

"Mac, it is. Are you ready to leave?"

I glanced at Giselle.

"I know these people are strangers to you, Callie, but we have carefully vetted and selected them to be your adoptive parents. You will live with them for the next six months. During that time, I'll visit regularly and if everything works out, the official papers will be signed making them your legal parents."

"What happens if they decide they don't want me?" The thought of being shuffled from foster home to foster home terrified me.

Mother crouched down and gathered my hands into hers. "Honey, we have waited a very long time for a child to call our own, we aren't going to decide we don't want you."

Her soothing, gentle voice set me at ease and I felt myself relax. I turned to Mac. "I'm ready."

He smiled broadly. "Let our new lives begin."

They each gathered one of my hands and after bidding Giselle goodbye, we left the office to head home. *Home,* would it be everything I'd dreamed of?

Chapter Two

CALLIE

I stood wedged between Mr. and Mrs. McKenzie staring up at the imposing building in front of me. This was to be my new home after three months of misery in a foster home. The woman who had birthed me was dead and no-one had any idea who my father was.

I was small for my age, being neglected and underfed has slowed down my growth. I've known for a long time, I wasn't 'normal'. My blue eyes were too big for my face -the reason why I was nicknamed *bug eyes* at school, my cheeks were hollow and sharp, my hair limp and dull. I was skinny to the point of being bony. I was hoping things will improve for me here.

Mother and Mac seemed kind and appeared to genuinely care about me. Time would tell, I guess.

On the way, we'd stopped at a nice restaurant and I was able to choose what I'd wanted to eat. I picked chicken smothered in gravy with lots of vegetables. A strange choice for a kid my age, but it's what I loved. For the first time in as long as I could remember, I had a full belly.

"What do you think of your new home, honey?" Mother smiled at me.

"It's very big." My voice was barely above a whisper.

"Come and have a look inside." Mac squeezed my hand and led me up the front steps to a huge wooden door.

He slid a key in the lock and pushed the door open wide. After he released my hand, he urged me inside. The place was like a palace where a princess would live. I'd thought homes like this only existed in magazines and books, not in real life.

Everything sparkled and gleamed in the light projected from the huge overhead chandelier. Before us was a sweeping staircase which seemed to beckon me to climb up to the clouds.

Mac left and strode off to our right.

"Follow me, honey." Mother headed to the stairs and proceeded upward.

When she realized I wasn't behind her, she turned and waited. I hurried to catch up and when I reached her, she gathered my hand and led me to the top of the steps. We swung to the left and stopped in front of a closed door. Mothers hand rested on the knob.

"If there is anything you don't like, we can change it."

I nodded before she swung the door open.

I placed my hands over my mouth and wondered if I'd stepped into some alternate universe. The room was straight off the pages of a fairytale book. Tentatively, I stepped forward.

The room was painted in pale pink and deep pink carpet covered the floor. The bed and other furnishings were white. The covering on the bed was white patterned with pink roses.

Shelves on the wall held a myriad of dolls and books, more than I'd known even existed. A desk under the large window had a laptop computer resting atop. A white chair sat before it. Curtains, which matched the bed covering, hung at the window. It was every girl's dream bedroom.

I turned and threw myself against mother in a hug. "Thank you mother, it's beautiful."

She patted the top of my red hair covered head and kissed my cheek before standing me away from her. "I expect you to take good care of everything."

"I promise, I'll keep everything as good as new."

"Your closet has new clothes, shoes, and school uniforms. You start at Foster Preparatory on Monday. I was told your grades are good."

"Straight A's. I love school especially English and Social Studies."

"You managed that while taking care of yourself."

"Yes."

Mother crouched down and hugged me. "I'm very proud of you."

I didn't know what to say. I wasn't used to praise and I certainly wasn't used to being hugged. It felt good.

She glanced at the gold watch on her wrist. "There are two hours before supper. Have a look around the house and gardens, but don't leave the grounds."

"I won't and thank you for wanting me."

She kissed my forehead before she spun on her heel and left the room.

****

I removed my coat and glanced around for a closet. I opened a white painted door on the wall opposite and I felt my eyes widen. Dozens of dresses, skirts, shirts and pants hung neatly in sections. I fingered the fabrics. Soft and silky, not hard and scratchy like I was used to. Every color of the rainbow appeared to be represented.

I pulled out the top drawer of a dresser to find neatly folded underwear. The drawer below held shirts in a myriad of colors. At the bottom were swimsuits and shorts. I closed the drawer and stood up. Off to one side were shelves containing sandals, flip flops, boots, sneakers and party shoes. I wanted for nothing. After closing the door, I moved to another door alongside. Surely it couldn't be another closet? I had enough clothes to last me a lifetime.

I twisted the knob and gasped with delight when the door opened to reveal my very own bathroom. Like the bedroom, it was painted in a soft pink with gleaming white fittings. The room was spotless, not even dust motes dared to dance in the last of the evening light which streamed through the window. I ran my fingers over the sink – no grime, no cracks, no mold. I must have died and gone to heaven.

I wrapped my arms around my thin waist as tears flowed over my cheeks. I'd never seen a bathroom so beautiful before and it was mine. All mine!

I pulled myself together and headed back to the bedroom, closing the door with a soft click. Moving closer, I examined the beautiful porcelain dolls. They would never be held, I would be terrified of dropping or dirtying them.

Feeling overwhelmed, I left the room and ventured downstairs. Mother was speaking with someone, I headed in the direction of her voice. It led me to the kitchen, I paused in the doorway and noted the white gleaming cupboards and stainless appliances.

Mother stood chopping vegetables while talking to a short, plump, elderly lady. The old lady turned and noticed me standing in the doorway, fidgeting nervously. She smiled as she approached me while wiping her hands on the apron she wore.

"Come in, child, we don't bite."

Mother turned and smiled. "Callie, come and meet Mrs. Hobson."

I held out my hand and spoke politely and curtsied as I'd been taught by Mrs. R. "Pleased to meet you, Mrs. Hobson."

The chubby lady glanced at mother, raised her eyebrows and burst into laughter. "Child, who the devil told you to curtsy?" Her eyes watered as she laughed.

I looked to mother, inwardly pleading for guidance. "Mother, Mrs. R said we must always curtsy when we meet older people and address them by their proper title. She said it shows respect."

Mrs. Hobson laughed again, a loud booming laughter. It wasn't at all feminine and I noted her ample belly shook out of control.

"Mother, stop it." My mother sounded exasperated.

"I'm sorry, but child, Mrs. R is stuck in the last century. While we expect good manners and behavior, we also expect you to behave like a normal young girl, don't we Rebecca?"

"That's right mother. Maybe Callie could call you Granny?"

Mrs. Hobson glanced at me and lifted one eyebrow. "Now, I know I'd like that, what about you, Callie?"

"I've never had a granny." I glanced at mother and smiled. "I'd like that very much."

"Granny it is then." The old woman swept me into her arms and peppered my face with kisses. I giggled and squirmed. I'd never been hugged and kissed like this before.

"What are you girls up to?" I jumped at the sound of Mac's booming voice from the doorway.

Granny spun me around. My back pressed against her soft belly and her arms wrapped firmly around me. "Mind your own business, son, this is girl's business."

Now I was confused. I turned my head and peered up at granny. "Are you Mac's mama?"

She kissed the tip of my nose. "I surely am. Your new daddy is my only child."

"What about his daddy?"

Sadness shadowed her eyes and she had a faraway look. "He died when Patrick was about your age."

"That's sad. My mama was shot in the bar where she worked. No-one knows who my daddy is."

Granny hugged me closer.

"Was your foster home good, Callie?" Mother asked anxiously.

"It was okay, they didn't beat me but I don't think they really wanted me. I think they only took me so they would have someone to do all the work around the house and for the money they got from the government."

Mac stepped further into the kitchen and crouched in front of me. He gathered my hands into his. "You're ours now, a McKenzie and you will never go without again. We expect you to do chores but you won't be a slave." He pulled me into his arms and hugged me tight. I'd never been happier.

Chapter Three

CALLIE

Life with mother and Mac was better than I ever dreamed it could be. They were kind, caring and loving. Giselle visited every week for the first month, but when I assured her I was happy, her visits reduced to once a month.

My fourteenth birthday was amazing. I'd made a few friends at my new school, not close friends who I hung out with after school, I was too quiet and shy. They were friends who sat with me at lunch, talked about their weekends and grumbled over siblings. They tried hard to include me and I was grateful, but I was still settling in to having a family who cared about me and wanted to spend every moment with them.

My school friends accepted the invitation to my party, the first of my life, a new experience for me. I received jewelry, music, cash and store cards. The school I attended was selective and students came from the wealthiest families in the city, my gifts were overly generous. I learned from mother, it didn't do to be outdone by another. I was glad she's not like that. From my parents I received more clothes, shoes, a matching bracelet and ring set and iPod shuffle.

Mother had decorated the back garden with streamers, balloons and fairy lights. Hundreds of pink roses had the flowers cut off and they floated on the surface of the pool. I'd never imagined anything like it, let alone seen it. It was entirely different world to the one I had previously lived in.

We laughed, ate, danced and I spoke to some boys. I missed my mom, but loved my new life.

Giselle attended my party and after everyone had left, she sat down with me and my parents. I had a bad feeling about it and tensed. She explained, Mac had been offered a prestigious position in his firm in a middle eastern country. It was worth a lot of money and was what he'd been working toward for a long time. He'd accepted the offer and was leaving in a little over a month.

Tears burned my eyes, I jumped up from my chair and screamed out, "I knew it was too good to last." I'd attempted to flee to my room but Mac grabbed my wrist, pulled me against his chest and held me while I cried.

When I'd settled a little, he tilted my chin up and wiped the tears from my face.

"Come and sit down and listen to us." He sat back on the chair and pulled me onto his lap, seated sideways, I was able to see all three adults.

Giselle spoke, "I've discussed this with your parents and although you have only been with them for three months, we have decided to petition for your adoption so you can go overseas with them. The judge will ask you if it's what you want, if it's not, you need to tell us now. If you don't want the McKenzie's to be your family, you'll be placed in a foster home while I search for another coupe willing to adopt a teenager.

I turned my face up to Mac. "I want you to adopt me, I want to go with you.

Mac kissed me gently and hugged me close. "Then, my darling, you shall become part of our family."

Giselle stood. "I'll organize the court papers and let you know when the date is set.

My parents thanked her and mother showed her to the door. Mac held me close, told me how happy he was and that he loved me.

"Mac?"

"Yes, baby girl."

"I've changed my mind, I'd like to call you, daddy."

Tears welled in his eyes and he hugged me close, I was so happy.

***

Excitement built as we awaited news of my court date. Mother and I spent time packing and getting ready to move. Granny had decided she didn't want to go with us as it was *"too darn hot for these old bones."* Daddy had arranged for her to move into a retirement village instead.

Mother and I were upstairs in my room dancing to *Pink* when a loud banging sounded at the front door. She turned down the music. "Keep packing that box, honey and I'll see who's at the door. Granny is next door with Mrs. Rains." She disappeared from my room and moments later I heard a blood-curdling scream.

I dropped what I'd been doing and raced downstairs, screeching to a halt near the front door. Two policemen helped mother into the living room. She was crying hysterically and kept repeating, "no, it's not possible."

One of the policemen looked at me with a helpless expression. I had no idea what to do or say, I didn't have a clue what had happened. So, I did the first thing which sprang to mind.

"I'll go and get granny."

I raced from the house as if the devil himself was after me, jumped the side fence to save time and hurried to the back porch. I knew it was where I'd find granny helping her friend with the herb garden.

I tugged at granny's arm. "Granny, granny, come quick. Something's happened. The police are here and mother's crying. I grabbed her hand and tugged.

"For heaven sake child, I'm coming."

The trip back to the house seemed to take forever, granny wasn't the fastest mover on Earth. When we reached the living room and mother saw granny, she stood and threw herself into the old woman's arms. As mother sobbed, one of the policemen explained what had happened to granny. Mac had been hit and killed by a drunk driver, he'd died instantly.

I stood rooted to the spot. I didn't scream. I didn't cry. I didn't make a sound. Instead, I found my feet, slowly backed out of the room and rushed upstairs to my room where I threw myself onto the bed and screamed into my pillow.

I don't know how long I lay on my bed, screaming, kicking, crying. I wanted daddy back, he couldn't be dead, I loved him. If I didn't believe it, it couldn't be true.

I felt a hand touch my back, rolled over and sat up to find granny perched on the edge of the bed. Her face was tear-stained, her eyes heavy with devastation. I flung myself into her arms.

"He can't be dead, granny. I love him so much. I want him back. Bring him back now," I screamed like a child throwing a tantrum. I raised my head from her chest and gazed into her eyes. "Please granny, tell them they're wrong. Tell them it's a mistake and my daddy is okay. He'll be home soon."

Fresh tears assaulted her eyes. "Oh, honey, I wish I could. They showed me pictures, your daddy won't be coming home."

We held each other and cried until exhaustion overtook me and I fell asleep in her arms.

It was the middle of the night when I woke and I recalled what had happened. I climbed from the bed, crept down the hall and slipped under the covers with mother. She gathered me into her arms and kissed my forehead.

"Are you hungry, honey?"

"No, mother. I just want you to hold me. I miss daddy."

"I do too, come here."

I snuggled into her, arms wrapped around me and fell into a troubled sleep.

***

The day after daddy's funeral, a week later, Giselle turned up at the house with a man called Ray Marker. She had called and told mother she needed to speak with us urgently. Mother invited them in and we all sat in the living room. Me, sandwiched between mother and granny. Ray and Giselle in chairs opposite. I studied the man.

He had a mean face, and tiny eyes which seemed to be darting all around. The clothes he wore were old and wrinkled, his hair hadn't seen a comb for a long while. I didn't like him and wondered why he was here.

Giselle didn't seem her usual self and I felt sick to my stomach; something was terribly wrong.

"Callie, Ray is your birth mother's cousin. He just found out about her death and as your next of kin, he's claiming custodial rights over you."

"No, I'm not leaving here." I held onto mother with a death grip.

"Honey, he applied to the court and he's been granted full custody. You have to go with him."

I felt mother and granny trembling beside me, the sneer on his face caused bile to bubble up in my throat.

"I don't care what the court said, I'm not going with him."

Mother and granny wrapped me in their arms and I felt safe and protected, they wouldn't allow this man to take me away from them.

"I won't allow it," Mother said defiantly. "I'll take it back to court. She's my daughter now."

"Rebecca, I'm sorry, the court won't grant you custody over a family member."

"They have to, I'll tell the judge," I cried.

Giselle gave me a sad look. "I'm sorry honey, I spoke to the judge on your behalf. Told him you were settled here, in a good school and recommended the adoption go ahead as planned. He refused."

"I'll run away." There was no way I was going anywhere with this man.

"Come on, darlin', I'm not that bad. I'll take care of ya and I have two little ones who ain't got a ma. They'd love a big sister."

"Callie, I'm sorry, but you have to go with Ray."

"Where do you live?" I hoped it was close by so I could still visit with mother and granny.

"On a farm at Malinga, two days drive from here. You'll have to do ya schoolin' from home, the nearest one is more than a hundred miles away. Nearest neighbor is about fifty miles down the road. You'll be able to learn to ride a horse, spend time with the animals."

An ominous feeling washed over me. I was being backed into a corner and couldn't do a damn thing about it.

Chapter Four

CALLIE

The trip to my new home took two days in Ray's beat up truck. We slept in the back on thin blankets because he said hotels were only for rich people, not poor farmers like him. We ate a small meal at a run-down diner and he made me pee in the bush. Ray wasn't a talker, and I was suffering with a broken heart, my separation from mother and granny was devastating. I'd promised mother that at the age of eighteen, legally an adult, I'd be back. It gave us both something to look forward to in the future. I sat silently, peering through the window, watching as the miles sped by.

It was late afternoon when we reached the farm. It was, as he'd said, out in the middle of nowhere. Chickens, ducks and goats milled around the front of a building, a broken-down shack and on the dilapidated porch. The shack leaned at a dangerous angle and was in need of a great deal of repair.

"Looks like the place needs a lot of fixing."

The slap to my face knocked my head against the window, my lip split and I tasted blood on my tongue. I held a hand to my now stinging cheek and fought back tears.

"You're gonna learn how to speak to me with respect, bitch, or you're gonna wish you'd never been born. Now, grab your bag, get in the house and make us supper while I take care of the animals.

I was a quick learner and didn't say a word. I climbed from the truck, grabbed my suitcase from the back of the truck, and trudged onto the porch.

When I opened the door and stepped inside, I suspected I'd stepped straight into Hell.

***

After placing my suitcase on the floor, I studied the room. *One* room. The *only* room. At one end was a crude, minimal kitchen, a small dining table with two chairs, and a battered sofa. At the other end, a bed and small closet. *One* bed. I felt sick. Glancing around, I wondered—where were the little ones Ray had spoken about?

I shrugged, figuring I'd find out sooner or later. I moved my suitcase to the end of the bed and crossed back to the kitchen where I rummaged through cupboards and the fridge until I found the ingredients to make a beef stew. I'd just set the pot onto the cooker when Ray sauntered in.

"What are we having?"

"Beef stew, it'll be a while if you have something you need to do."

He nodded before disappearing back outside. I opened the suitcase, hung a few clothes on the side of the closet and left others folded inside due to the lack of drawers. When Ray came back an hour later, he was carrying a cot and a mattress. I breathed a loud sigh of relief when he moved the dining table aside and set it up near the kitchen.

"Ain't much room but it'll do."

I dished up our meal and we sat down at the table. Ray forked meat and vegetables into his mouth and gobbled it down noisily.

"Damn, you can cook. This is good."

"Granny taught me."

Ray nodded, more interested in stuffing food into his mouth than talking.

"Where are the little ones?"

"They live with my wife's sister. I told that Giselle woman and the judge they lived here to get some sympathy."

"How did your wife die?"

"Fell and hit her head."

Pushed more like it. My eyes darted to the larger bed and back to Ray. He'd seen my anxious glance and smirked, my stomach somersaulted.

"Don't fret, I ain't no rapist, I'll never touch ya in that way. I have a temper though and don't like it when people don't do as I say."

I breathed a sigh of relief. I believed him. I didn't like him, but believed he was telling the truth. Over supper he told me what my chores would be and what was expected of me. I'd thought I was a slave at my first foster home, I was wrong. It was a picnic compared to what awaited me here.

"How do we get supplies?" I was hoping it might present an avenue of escape.

"*I* get the supplies once a month. Town is two hours from here and you won't be going so don't go getting any ideas."

Ray had lied about many things to mother and Giselle. There were no little ones, no school and no horse to ride. I wondered if he was really my mother's cousin, but I wasn't stupid enough to ask.

There was only backbreaking work from dawn through to dusk, supper, cleaning and bed. I fell into an exhausted sleep every night.

I'd been screamed at, slapped across the backside, the face and repeatedly called a bitch when I didn't do something quite right, but worse was yet to come. Three weeks after I'd arrived, I felt unwell and didn't get out of bed to make breakfast while Ray was out milking the cow. When he returned and found me lying in bed, he grabbed a fistful of hair and threw me into the kitchen. My head hit the cupboard and I sat on the floor, stunned. He crouched before me, rage causing his face to turn almost purple, veins so strained they looked ready to burst.

"When I go out to milk, you get your fucking ass out of bed and make breakfast. Is that clear?" It was the first time I'd seen Ray in such a rage and it terrified me. This was no ordinary anger.

"I don't feel well," I whispered.

His fist hit the side of my face and I heard a loud crack, I screamed out in pain.

"Wrong fucking answer."

He punched me in the stomach and I doubled over in agony.

"I can keep this up all fucking day, until you answer me. AM I FUCKING CLEAR?"

I nodded and squeaked out a yes.

"Good, now get your fucking ass up and make breakfast."

My face throbbed and I was losing vision as my face swelled, my stomach was agonizing. I felt bile burning its way up my throat and before I could stop myself, I puked all over the front of Ray's shirt. He let out a roar of anger, picked me up like a rag doll and flung me to the other side of the room. My head crashed against the wall and darkness engulfed me.

Several hours later, I woke on my cot. Every part of me throbbed and screamed in pain.

"Good you're awake, get up bitch and make my supper."

I have no idea how I dragged myself from the bed and stayed on my feet long enough to make him supper, but I did. No matter how many ferocious beatings I took, I always managed to make him a meal.

For the following two years, I was not only Ray's slave but his personal punching bag. God only knows how many bones I'd had broken. No matter how badly I was hurt, I never once saw a doctor. The one thing I was grateful for—he never once attempted to force himself on me in a sexual way.

***

My seventeenth birthday had passed and eighteen was approaching fast. I again had what I suspected was a broken arm and a face so swollen

I was barely able to see. Ray had taken to making, and drinking, rotgut whiskey. His rages were more frequent and a hell of lot more vicious. I knew I had to get away or I'd end up dead. I waited until he was out cold the following night before slipping away. I had no idea which direction to head in, but hoped I'd find a main road and maybe someone would pick me up.

Barefooted, wearing only a dress that was three times too big; I set out. I was nothing more than skin and bones. My original clothes were long gone, as were my underwear and shoes. I was having to wear Ray's wife's dresses now. I slunk through the woods at the back of the shack supporting my swollen, limp arm. I knew the road to town was via the way I'd come in two years before, but there was no cover, nowhere to hide. I weaved in and out of trees, confident I wasn't being followed, Ray was too drunk. Ignoring the sounds of creatures protesting at being disturbed, and the pain in my feet when I stepped on a sharp rock or thorny branch, I pushed on for hours. Barely able to see and having no clue where I was. Exhausted, but too frightened to stop.

Hearing the distant rumble of a motorcycle caused my breath to hitch and heart to thump erratically. I headed toward the sound, stumbling from the trees and onto a road. I'd found a road! Turning toward the sound, I was blinded by the beautiful sight of a headlight. I jumped up and down, shouting for the rider to stop. To my relief, the bike started to slow and came to a stop.

***

The man tilted his visor up, but in the pale moonlight I couldn't see the features of his face. He was big, that much I could tell. One foot rested easily on the ground as the bike continued to rumble beneath him. He looked me up and down and said, "get on and hang on." It appeared he was a man of few words.

He flipped down his visor and I scrambled up behind him, wrapping one arm around his waist. What did I have to lose? If he took me out to some isolated spot and killed me, I'd be no worse off than I currently was. Even through his leather jacket I could feel the hardness of his muscles. I rested my broken arm in my lap and hung on for dear life as he accelerated the bike down the dark road.

For a reason I couldn't explain, I felt safe. The cold wind whipping past as the bike ate up the miles taking me further away from Ray. I lay my head on the man's back and closed my eyes. Although I wanted to sleep, was cold, in need of a meal, and decent night's sleep, I stayed alert. I really didn't want to fall off and become one with the road.

The bike hummed beneath us, and despite my best intentions, I drifted off. I woke with a start when I felt a strong grip on my arm because I'd been slipping. I shifted my ass back onto the seat and sat upright to keep myself awake. The man released the grip on my arm.

We rode throughout the night, and as the sun poked its head over the horizon, he slowed and turned the bike onto a dirt track. I know I should have felt frightened. A strange man was taking me along what appeared to be an isolated road, but I wasn't. To be honest, I was past caring. If he decided to rape, and kill me, I'd be freed from this miserable life. I figured whatever waited for me in the afterlife couldn't possibly be worse than what I had in this one.

After a few miles, he brought the bike to a stop in front of a pretty, well-kept cottage. Two small children erupted from the front door and dashed toward us. I climbed off the bike and stood aside. The man stepped off and kicked out the side stand.

I examined the detail on the back of his jacket—the head of a wolf leaning over the front of a motorcycle and the words—*Free Lords MC Foster.*

Great, I'd landed in the arms of a man who was part of a motorcycle gang. I raised my eyes to the sky. *Enough already. Just kill me and be done with it, will ya?*

The man removed his jacket, folded it over the seat of his bike, and placed his helmet on top. Holy shit, the man was a fucking mountain. His long legs were encased in black leather pants and he wore knee length boots. A black t-shirt with rolled up sleeves showed off his muscular arms. Down his right arm was a tattoo, the same as the image on the back of his jacket.

Two little girls launched themselves at him screaming, "Uncle Jake." After scooping one into each arm, they wrapped their arms around his neck and peppered his face with kisses.

Maybe I wasn't going to die after all. Surely, anyone who loved children as this man appeared to, and who children seemed to love, couldn't be all bad. I stood watching while Jake asked them about school and their ponies. They chattered excitedly until one noticed me.

"Who's the girl, uncle Jake?" one asked. "Why is she bleeding?"

Jake placed the girls onto the ground and strode toward me. "What the fuck? Who did this to you?"

He pointed at the cuts, bruises, and strange angle of my arm. Being daylight he was now able to see the extent of my injuries, and by the look on his face, he wanted to kill whoever had hurt me.

My stomach chose that moment to grumble, I felt woozy, and before I could answer, darkness engulfed me.

Chapter Five

JAKE

I swept the kid into my arms before she hit the ground, she looked like she'd been hit by a fucking truck.

"Rosy, Ella, run inside and tell mama I've got a kid who's hurt."

My nieces set off running, and the screen door slammed with an almighty bang as they charged into the house. I heard them screaming out for their mama. Hell, the whole fucking countryside could have heard them.

I carried the kid up to the house, and my sister, Maree, caught up with me as I shoved through the door.

"Take her through to Ella's room, she can share with Rosy. What happened? Who is she?"

"No idea, found her in the middle of the road about four hundred miles back, didn't realize she was beat-up until we got here. If I'd known, I would have stopped off at a hotel and let her rest."

"Look at how she's dressed, she must be half frozen. What were you thinking little brother?"

"I couldn't see much, it was dark, and I figured if she hugged into me she'd stay warm."

"Jake, I swear sometimes you don't have the God given brains you were born with."

Maree pulled back the bed covers and I set the kid onto the sheet. My sister pushed me out of the way to take a closer look. She lifted the girl's hand and glared at me.

"Her dress is so thin she might as well be wearing nothing, she's icy cold. Help me get it off and we'll wrap a blanket around her. We need to get her warm."

I helped Maree get rid of the filthy, threadbare dress, and while she gasped, my stomach turned over.

"Someone's used her face as a punching bag and it's not too long ago. I've never seen so much swelling and bruising. Look at her arms and legs—cuts and bruises everywhere. I don't think she's had a decent feed in a very long time. Her poor feet are cut to pieces, and I'll need to remove the thorns. She's a mess, Jake. Probably trying to escape from somewhere when you found her."

I pointed to the kid's arm. "Look at her arm, does it look strange to you?"

Maree felt along the length and frowned. "Broken, pretty badly I'd say. We need Doc Windsor."

"That's why she only held on with one arm, I thought maybe she was used to bikes, but I can see now that wasn't the case."

"It's been a long time since she's had a decent meal, she's so thin."

My sister was right, the girl was skin and bone. I mean, I've seen skinny models, and movie stars but compared to this kid, they were downright fat.

"How old do you reckon she is, sis?"

"Hmm, ten, eleven maybe, judging by the lack of development. Her breasts haven't appeared yet and she has no pubic hair."

"Who the fuck would do this?"

"I don't know, Jake, but I'd like to put a bullet in the asshole."

"Mama, is she hurt bad?"

Marie and I both jumped at the sound of Ella's voice, and Maree hurriedly pulled the covers over the girl. We hadn't realized the twins had followed us into the room. This was no sight for seven-year-old kids. Fuck, it wasn't a sight for me and I was twenty-three.

"Girls, go into the living room and play."

My nieces, being the gorgeous, obedient little dolls they were, immediately left the room.

"What do you think we should do?" I asked my big sister. She was twelve years older than me and I'd always looked up to her. I was worried, if this kid was on the run, and we took her to the hospital, the asshole who'd beaten her would no doubt come after her again.

"Mitch is out bringing in stock, can you go into town and ask Doc to come out here? We'll be guided by what he says."

"No hospital, he'll find me. He can't know where I am." The voice was barely above a whisper, but we both heard her speak. Maree moved closer and gathered her hand.

"Honey, you're awake. My name's Maree and this big lug..." She pointed at where I stood. "...who almost froze you to death, is my little brother, Jake."

"He don't look so little. I'm Callie, and I don't mind, he saved my ass."

"You're safe here, honey. How old are you?"

"Seventeen, eighteen soon."

I stepped back, reeling in shock. This tiny, underdeveloped, half-starved kid was almost eighteen? She should have looked like a woman. My eyes darted to Maree and I saw she was every bit as shocked as I felt.

"I'm going to send Jake into Foster for our doctor. You can trust him. You have a badly broken arm and need stitches in your feet. We won't allow you to be taken back, I promise."

"I stepped on rocks and thorns in the woods when I was escaping. Foster? But Ray's place was two days from there and we were only on the road for one night."

"He probably took you a longer way so you'd think you were further from town than you really were. Foster is about fifteen minutes from here."

"May I have some water, please?"

"Of course, honey." Maree glanced my way.

I hurried through to the kitchen, noting the girls were playing with their dolls in the living room. Rosy looked up as I passed. "Will she be okay, Uncle Jake?"

"Doc will fix her," I assured before taking a pitcher of cold water from the fridge and filling a glass.

With the pitcher back where it came from, I returned to the bedroom and handed the glass to Maree. I supported Callie's back, helping her to sit forward, and Maree held the glass to her lips. She drank thirstily before becoming limp. I set her back against the pillows and pulled the covers back up to her chin.

"I'll let the sheriff know." I wanted the bastard hung, drawn and quartered.

"No!" Callie's eyes filled with terror. "It's my word against his, they'll make me go back."

"I think your word will be a hell of a lot more powerful than his when the sheriff takes a look at you," I growled.

Maree sat on the edge of the bed and gathered Callie's hand again. I was so proud of my sister, she knew what to do when it was needed.

"Who did this to you, honey?"

"My mother's cousin. This isn't as bad as some of the other times."

Maree and I glanced at each other. My fists clenched. I wanted to kill the asshole. Fuck, if she'd been worse than this, how had she managed to survive?

"How long has this been going on?" I know I sounded angry.

Callie trembled, and pushed herself back against the pillows, tears streamed from her eyes. I'd seen this in abuse victims before—the cowering away, waiting for the strike of a hand. I moved closer and ran my hand down her arm, careful not to cause pain.

"Sweetheart, I'm not angry with you, I'm angry at the asshole who did this. She visibly relaxed at my words. "I'll go and fetch Doc, but won't say anything to the sheriff. Maybe I'll take care of this myself."

I patted her hand and strode from the room. If I'd known she was in such bad shape when I stopped to pick her up, I would have forced her to show me where the asshole lived and beaten the crap out of him. Never mind, his time will come.

***

CALLIE

I wasn't sure how I'd ended up inside the house, in the softest bed I'd been in for almost three years. Despite my pain, it felt wonderful. I had no idea why I was naked and frankly, I didn't give a fuck. I just wanted to sleep and never wake up.

Jake had frightened me when he became angry, I was waiting for the punches to start. But, when he'd quietly spoken, reassuring me, I realized I'd misjudged him. After he'd left, his sister questioned me. She had warm brown eyes like mothers and I instinctively knew I could trust her.

"How are you feeling, honey?"

"Tired, sick, in pain." I wasn't going to sugarcoat it. "I feel like shit, but I'll be fine to move on in a couple of days unless you want me out of here now. I don't want to be in the way."

Maree clutched my hand. "You're not in the way. You'll be staying until your injuries are healed and we fatten you up. Do you have somewhere you can go when you're well?"

"Maybe. I was to be adopted when Ray came for me. I think mother and granny would take me back."

"Why were you with Ray?"

"I was only fourteen. Mac, who was to be my adoptive daddy was killed in a car accident. The judge said mother couldn't have me because she was on her own and Ray was my next of kin. I didn't want to go, but they threatened mother with arrest if I didn't."

"I know you're tired, and I'm asking a lot of questions, but honey, Jake won't let this rest. He was on his way back from a meeting with the Roma chapter and was going to stay here for a week before he went home to his club. I can guarantee you, he'll round up his VP and a couple of the others, and they'll pay Ray a visit he won't forget."

"Club?"

"Jake is President of the Free Lords Motorcycle Club in Foster. He owns a couple of workshops in town, where he's a mechanic."

"Drugs, guns?"

"No, it was daddy's club before Jake was elected, and neither them, nor their members, tolerate anything illegal. At least I don't think they do. They're at war with the Panthers from Corgette which worries me a lot. Apparently, Julio wants to move in Free Lords territory to deal drugs and guns. I'm scared to death it will turn into all-out war and Jake will be hurt. Jake doesn't say much about club business, so I don't know the facts, only what I hear on the streets."

My eyes began drifting shut although I wanted to know more about my knight on a shining *Harley*.

Maree patted my hand. "Get some rest, honey. Doc will be here in about an hour. I'll make sure the girls stay quiet."

Before she'd left the room, I'd drifted into a deep sleep.

***

A soft hand running down the side of my face woke me. I opened my eyes to see a kindly old man smiling down at me.

"Hello, Miss. I'm Doc Windsor. I can see you've been in the wars. Can I check out your injuries?"

I nodded, still half asleep. Maree hovered close by, the only other person in the room.

"First off, let's check this arm. Has it been broken before?"

"Both arms have been, too many times to remember."

"Why didn't your doctor report it to the authorities?"

"Didn't see one. I made do with a tree branch and rags. Ray wouldn't let me see anyone. He said if I was left with a crooked arm, it served me right." I screamed when he squeezed my arm a little below the elbow even though he had the gentlest of touches. Tears sprang to my eyes. He let go immediately and stepped back.

"You've got a bad break, I suspect you need surgery."

"No!"

Maree moved closer and gathered my hand. "Honey, you need to be in the hospital, Doc can't fix you here."

"I have no money and he'll find me."

"Don't worry about that. Jake is taking care of the bills and he'll stay with you so you're safe." Maree attempted to assure me.

"I have no way of paying him back."

"Don't worry about that now, you need to get well."

I turned to the doctor. "Is it really necessary?"

Doc nodded. "I'm afraid it is. You're in quite a bad way. I'd like to do scans, x-rays, and tests to see how much damage has been done over the past years."

I sighed. Too sick, and too tired to argue. "I'll need my dress, I'm not going anywhere naked."

Maree held up a bag. "Jake picked up underwear, nightgowns, a robe and slippers when he went into town to fetch Doc."

While Doc left the room to speak with Jake, Maree helped me into panties and a powder blue nightgown. The fabric was whisper soft against my bruised skin.

Jake entered the room a few moments later with Doc. He helped Maree to sit me on the side of the bed. steadying me when I became dizzy and swayed. Together, they slipped the robe on and pulled the fluffy slippers onto my feet.

"I'm borrowing Maree's car to take you into the hospital in Foster." Jake turned to his sister. "I'll stay with her until I know what's going on, so don't worry about supper for me, I'll grab something in town. If Callie does need surgery, while she's in theater, I'll head to the clubhouse and organize some of the members to be at the hospital in shifts around the clock." He turned back to me. "You won't be left alone at any time."

"Thank you for everything, Jake."

He slipped one arm behind my back, the other under my knees, and lifted me as if I weighed nothing. Probably because I didn't.

When we reached the sedan parked by the front door, Jake lowered me into the passenger seat and strapped on the belt.

Maree leaned in, kissed my cheek and promised to visit. Jake climbed behind the wheel, and after Doc said he'd meet us at the hospital, he started the motor and slowly eased away.

Chapter Six

CALLIE

I didn't remember the trip to the hospital, I'd slept all the way. Not opening my eyes until Jake's arms slipped around my waist, under both legs, and I was lifted from the car. He strode into the hospital through a pair of sliding glass doors and up to a desk where a nurse eyed him with disgust.

"Dr. Windsor sent me."

She continued looking at Jake like he was something she'd stepped in. "Name?"

"Callie McKenzie and he didn't do this." I snapped angrily.

I don't know why I felt the need to say something. I guess I hated her thinking this kind man was responsible for my injuries. Her demeanor changed instantly and she smiled.

"Bring her through and I'll send the doctor in as soon as he arrives. In the meantime, I have paperwork which needs to be filled out."

We followed her through a door and into a room with a cot along one wall. Monitors and other machinery were everywhere.

Jake laid me on the bed, and the nurse handed a clipboard to him, before helping me out of my nightgown, robe and slippers, and into a hospital gown. After covering me with a sheet, she left the room. Jake took a seat by the bed.

He sat with pen poised over the sheet of paper attached to the clipboard. We filled it in as best we could as there were a lot of questions I couldn't answer. Like, 'address' for example—I didn't have one. Jake told me not to worry and put his address on the sheet. Once done, he set the clipboard aside and leaned forward.

"How are you feeling now, honey?"

"Tired mostly. Shouldn't you be at work?"

"Nope, took a week off to spend time with my sister and the girls. VP is looking after things. Once you go up for surgery, I'll go and talk to them about having someone here around the clock."

I felt disappointed that Jake wasn't going to be with me all the time but shrugged it off. The last thing I needed was a crush. "How long have you been in the club?"

"All my life. Dad was President so Maree and I grew up with it."

"Where's your dad now?"

"Him and ma moved to Florida where it's warmer. They visit a couple of times a year. Ma has bad arthritis and the warm weather helps ease the pain."

Before I could ask anything else, Doc Windsor entered the cubicle with a nurse. They both stepped closer to the bed.

"Callie, I'm going to book a range of tests and have an Orthopedic Specialist come down to check your arm after it's x-rayed. He'll be the one to operate. Karen will clean up, and dress your wounds, and I'll be back a little later."

"Thank you, Dr. Windsor."

"Doc is just fine and you're welcome sweetheart." He patted my hand before leaving.

Jake helped Karen change me into a hospital gown and I felt my bruised face heating. For some unexplained reason, he was the last person I wanted looking at my scrawny body. My clothes were placed into a brown paper bag and handed to Jake.

***

The rest of the day was exhausting. Full body scan, multiple x-rays, pee test, blood test, and stitches to both feet. I thought it would never end and the pain was becoming unbearable. Through it all, Jake stayed by my side. I had just started to doze when Doc and another man in a white coat entered the room.

Doc carried a folder in his hands and spoke first. "We have your results, would you like Jake to leave so we can discuss them privately?"

I gazed into Jake's eyes, they resembled melted chocolate with golden threads that sparkled when hit with the fluorescent light. I really liked him. I felt safe with him nearby. "No, I'd like him to stay if he doesn't mind."

"I don't mind," Jake agreed. He leaned forward and held my hand.

"Very well. First off, this is Dr. Blume and he's having theater prepared for your surgery. You'll be going up shortly."

Dr. Blume was a bear of a man, almost as big as Jake, with rich brown skin and smiling eyes. I liked him immediately. When he spoke, his voice was soft and kind. "Callie, your arm is badly broken in three places. There is a great deal of scar tissue from previous breaks and that will be cleaned up during surgery. Doc Windsor tells me, you received no treatment for previous breaks which explains why your arm is misaligned. I'll be inserting pins and a plate to help you regain strength and the use of your arm. You'll have a cast on for six weeks and then you'll need therapy to bring back movement. It will be a long, slow process I'm afraid."

Great, fucking great. How was I going to live without the use of one arm? Hopefully mother and granny would still be at the house and able to take me back. I couldn't impose on Maree for that length of time.

"I'll see you upstairs," Dr. Blume said before leaving.

Doc continued., "You have numerous old breaks, Callie. Several in both arms, your pelvis, almost every rib has been broken at some stage, collarbones, and cheeks. I have no idea what you've been through, but from studying the scans, and x-rays, you've endured a great deal of suffering. I've treated a lot of abuse victims in my time, but you would be one of the worst. To be frank, I'm surprised you didn't commit suicide before now."

"I guess I have a strong will to live, Doc."

He nodded. "You certainly must. Your blood tests show you are malnourished, but we didn't need tests to know that. You have the development of a ten-year-old and dangerously low levels of iron and other vitamins." He faced Jake. "She'll be here for a least a week, depending on how she responds to treatment. I'm going to set up a couple of I.V.s to get this young lady on the road to recovery."

"Do whatever you need to, Doc. I've spoken with the club members and they have agreed to foot the bill for all her treatment. I'll have someone with her at all times until she's ready to take back to Maree's where she'll be taken care of until she's well."

"I'll leave you now and organize to have everything set up in theater."

"Thank you, Doc," I murmured.

Karen gave me what she said was a pre-med to help me relax before surgery and shoved a funny paper hat on my head. Shortly after, a man came in and explained he was here to help Karen wheel me upstairs in the bed.

Jake kissed my forehead and moved out of their way. I enjoyed the kiss, his lips were warm and made me feel tingly. He promised he'd be there waiting when I came back.

***

I woke to the incessant beeping of machines and a thunderous headache. I turned my eyes, very slowly I might say, toward the sound of soft snoring. Jake was seated in a chair beside the bed, his long legs stretched out, and he was sound asleep.

My arm was in a cast and held up in the air attached to a pole. It ached like hell and I wanted it down. When I wriggled to unfasten the cloth holding the arm, Jake's eyes snapped open.

He leaned forward and placed his hand over mine. "What are you doing, sweetheart?"

"My arm aches, I hate having it up there. I want it down."

"Leave it be and I'll fetch the nurse."

He left the room and moments later returned with a nurse.

"I hear your arm's aching?" She moved to where my arm was strung up and felt my fingers. I have no idea why, I was sure there was no blood left in them. "Dr. Blume gave us permission to take it down six hours post-surgery if it was aching and it's been almost seven."

"Seven hours?"

"Yes." She unpinned the cloth holding my arm and lowered it onto a spare pillow on the bed, it gave me almost instant relief.

My fingers tingled as blood rushed back. I glanced at Jake. "You must be worn out, go home."

"I'm fine, I'll go home in the morning when Nose comes in. He'll keep watch over you while I grab some sleep."

The nurse checked the position of my arm on the pillow, checked my temperature, and left the room.

"Nose, who calls their son, Nose? Did his mother not like him?"

Jake laughed and I giggled. "It's his nickname because he can smell drugs from across the room."

"What's yours?"

"Bear."

"Bear?"

"Yep, because I'm so big."

"Makes sense. Seriously, Jake, thank you. I don't know what I would have done if you hadn't stopped and picked me up."

He nodded and looked thoughtful. "I need to know where Ray lives, Callie. He can't be allowed to get away with what he's done to you. You must have been through fucking hell. Hearing about your past injuries makes my fucking blood boil."

I remembered what Maree had said about Jake not giving up until he'd taught Ray a lesson. Did I want Ray beaten to a pulp? I had no illusion that's what would happen when Jake and his men found him.

"I'll find him with, or without, your help, babe. I know where I found you and there aren't a lot of properties in that area."

"Jake, honestly I don't know the address. I never left the place but I can try and explain where it is." Yeah, I wanted Ray to pay for the hell he'd put me through.

"You never left there? I can't believe you never once left the property."

I lifted a hand to my face. "Do you really think Ray would have let other people see me like this? And, I was beat up pretty much the whole time I was there."

Jake gathered my hand and squeezed, fuck it felt good having his warm hand wrapped around mine. I might look like a ten-year-old but I had the feelings of an eighteen-year-old.

"I'm so sorry that asshole hurt you, I'll make sure he never hurts anyone else."

I smiled before drifting off.

***

The week I was in hospital passed quickly and Jake visited every day. It was the highlight of my day. He'd help me into a wheelchair and wheel me around the hospital grounds. I was becoming very attached to him. When he wasn't there, one of his men from the club was. Despite their strange names—Nose, Picnic, Doc Ink, and Slider with his wife, Hotpants Sally, they turned out to be very nice, down to earth people. Not at all like I imagined bikers would be. They brought me books, flowers and chocolate. Doc Ink, even promised to give me a few tattoos once I was well enough and I couldn't wait to decorate my skin.

Maree and the girls also visited a couple of times, bringing me cake and straggly flowers which the little girls had picked from their garden. I was happy but cautious. I wasn't sure how long I'd have these people around me.

I was feeling much stronger, the bruises were healing, and the stitches had been removed. Doc Windsor said I'd put on a few pounds and he was happy with my progress, so I could leave. The day finally arrived and I was excited. As promised, Jake came for me. He bought me new underwear, a pair of jeans and a striped top. The nurse helped me dress, put the slippers on my feet, and helped me into a wheelchair. My arm was supported in a sling.

Jake returned to the room, we thanked the young nurse, and he wheeled me to the car which he'd parked by the front door. I was thrilled to be out of the hospital but was dreading him leaving the following day. I had to admit, I'd developed one hell of a crush on the tall, sexy biker. He lifted me into the car, strapped me in, and rounded the car to climb into the driver's seat.

"Maree said you can stay as long as you need. Are you sure you don't want me to take you around to your mother's?"

"No, I'm excited about seeing her and granny, but I don't want them seeing me like this. I don't want them to feel bad about not fighting harder to keep me."

"When you're ready, let me know and I'll take you."

"Thank you. How long will you be gone?"

"Only a couple of days."

"Are you going to kill Ray?"

"No, we don't kill. We will make him sorry he was born though." He paused and sucked in a deep breath. "Callie, there's one question I haven't asked. I know Doc would have but he wouldn't have breached your confidence to tell us...."

"No, Jake, Ray didn't sexually assault me."

His hands relaxed on the steering wheel and the tenseness left his shoulders.

"He never attempted to touch me that way, never even attempted to kiss me. He said he'd been married and had children, but he told me so many lies, I didn't believe it. I honestly think he's gay, although he never had another man over. I know I'm nothing to look at, but I find it strange he didn't try to rape me."

Jake glanced at me before concentrating back on the road. "You're a very pretty girl, Callie. Your cheeks are a bit sunken, but with more meat on your bones, they'll fill out. I reckon you're probably right about Ray. A man as cruel as he is, having you out in the middle of nowhere, he wouldn't have hesitated to rape you unless it's men he prefers."

"What about you, Jake. Girlfriend?"

"Nope. I've had a couple of relationships but they didn't work out."

Jake was very tight lipped about his past and it wasn't my place to insist he tell me.

"What will you do if your mother isn't in Foster? Will you still move there?"

"Yes, although I have no idea what I'll do. I haven't been to school since I was fourteen and can't afford to go back now. I'll have to try and find a job, maybe a check-out chick. At least it would give me money to get my own little place."

Jake followed the driveway to Maree's house and pulled the car up at the front. He switched off the motor and turned to me. "Don't you worry, my sweet Callie. I have a spare bedroom and you can live with me until you get on your feet."

My heart and stomach somersaulted as I imagined living with Jake. *Stop being so bloody ridiculous, he'll never be interested in a baby like you.*

Chapter Seven

CALLIE

“Maaa! Callie's here." Rosy charged down the front steps followed closely by Ella.

"I swear those girls get louder every day," Jake chuckled.

He wouldn't allow me to get out of the car on my own and swept me into his arms. I wasn't complaining. I rested my head against his chest and a small sigh escaped. Jake chuckled again and I felt my face heat.

Maree stepped from the house as Jake climbed the steps onto the porch. The girls followed us up.

"Welcome back, honey. I have your room ready."

"Thank you, but please, can I sit out here for a while. I'm so tired of being indoors and in bed."

Maree glanced at Jake. "I can't see why not, place her on the old porch couch, Jake. Ella, will you go inside and fetch a pillow, please?"

Both girls took off running inside, and Jake carried me to the other end of the porch where he lowered me onto the couch. It was a beautiful warm day with a gentle breeze blowing.

The screen door slammed with a bang loud enough to disturb the dead, and the girls came running, thumping like baby elephants on the wooden floor. Ella handed a pillow to me which Jake swiped before gently lifting my head and sliding it under.

Rosy proudly held up a throw blanket. "Mama, I got this in case Callie gets cold."

She draped it over me and smoothed out the wrinkles. I smiled and thanked her. These two little girls were adorable.

Jake stepped closer. "I'll leave you to it, I'm headed into Foster. I'll be back in a couple of days." He hugged and kissed his sister and then the girls. He crouched down beside me. "Take care of yourself, I expect to see some color in those cheeks when I return." He leaned forward and his warm lips kissed one of those cheeks. Every nerve in my body went haywire. I was in trouble, I had a serious crush on this man.

"Please be careful, Jake."

He patted my hand and grinned. "Always."

I watched as he strode to his bike, pulled on his jacket, and helmet, and threw a leg over the tank before settling onto the seat. A turn of the key and the bike rumbled to life beneath him. He waved before turning the bike onto the driveway and disappearing in a cloud of dust. I was going to miss him.

***

JAKE

I strode into the clubhouse where the men were gathered together, waiting for me, and dropped into a chair. Most members were present, a few remained holding down the fort at the workshops. Only Nose and Slider were coming with me to Moss County to deal with Ray, but I took the opportunity to discuss a few things with everyone.

"You men ready?" The two men knew who the question was directed at and nodded.

"As you all know by now, I picked up a young girl out in Moss County just over a week ago. Joker, Nose, Doc Ink, and Slider witnessed the state she was in, and according to doctors, she'd suffered even worse in the past. How the fuck she'd survived is anyone's guess. Doc rattled off so many broken bones, and injuries from the past, it made my fucking head spin. The first thing I wanted to do, was ride out there on my own and kill the asshole."

Nose spoke up while glancing at some of the other men. "You have no idea how bad she'd been beaten. While I watched over her at the hospital, I got talking to her. She's a sweet little thing, open and honest about the hell she's been through. The kid really needs a break. Like Pres, I wanted to jump on my bike, ride out there, and kill the fucker." Joker, Doc Ink, and Slider murmured their agreement.

"We won't be killing anyone, but the fucker won't be able to walk a straight line by the time we're finished with him. I had a long chat with Callie, she didn't know the address, but she showed me on a map where she thinks the property is. When I consider where I picked her up, I think she's right. She hadn't left the place in almost three years. On the way to the property, the bastard spent two days driving her all over the countryside so she wouldn't know where she was. Callie believed she was hours from anywhere when in fact she was only ten minutes from Lidcombe."

"Was she, you know.......?" VP asked.

"No, Callie said he never attempted to force himself on her. She suspects, and I agree, that he's gay. He was also careful not to damage her legs or arms too often so she could still do her chores."

"Damn, I would have enjoyed slicing his dick off,. Maybe I still will," Slider muttered.

There was a rumble of laughter. Slider was known for his expertise with a knife. As a guy on the streets before he joined the club, he would slide up to his victims, slice their throats, and slide away before they had a chance to fight back. Hence the nickname.

"No-one is cutting off dicks."

"Not *dicks*, Pres, only his. C'mon, be fair." Slider protested and another rumble of laughter erupted. Even I chuckled.

"Not *his* dick either. Now, moving onto business. Viking, how are the talks going with Julio?" Viking Dave was a tall, blonde, Danish American not much smaller in stature than me. He's also my VP and I'd trust him with my life.

"Julio is happy with our compromise to stay out of each other's business, but he's struggling to get it past the others at the club. As long as we keep our mouths shut about their business, he's happy. He doesn't want a turf war but some members are itching for it. They want our club and complete control of Foster. He insists he hasn't run drugs or guns into our territory."

I frowned, what we'd found had Panthers MC written all over it, so if not them, who? "Well, someone is fucking dealing and selling. I'm still convinced it's someone from the Panthers. Someone's gone rogue. Go back and tell Julio, the guns must have come into our territory from his club, there's no-one else in town capable of shifting the weapons. Someone is running behind his back. If they're dealing guns without him knowing, they'll be doing drugs too."

"I'll talk to him, see what we can do to help. I agree, someone in his midst is rogue, and if we don't stop it, there's gonna be all out war."

"Do what you need to get it sorted."

Viking nodded, and I had no doubt he would get to the bottom of things. Our club isn't squeaky clean. We've 'fixed' a few ruthless men, and done a few chop jobs in the shops, but for an MC club, we're reasonably law abiding. We also drink and party hard and share the odd woman. Hotpants Sally was one we shared until her and Slider fell in love; now she's off limits. Like my father before me, I don't tolerate drugs or gun running and if anyone mentions getting involved in either, they're out of the club. We all carry a piece but only for personal protection. Over the years, those into drugs, even if only for personal use have been booted from the club. I guess you could say we've made a few enemies. The members we have now respect me, and our charter. They know if they decide down the track to go in a different direction, they're free to leave.

"Ratchet, how are the shops? Any problems I should know about?" Ratchet was a qualified mechanic and one of the best people managers I know. He looks after both shops.

Another member, Psycho, an accountant, keeps all our books and pays our taxes. Yeah, Psycho, because he goes bat-shit crazy if the numbers don't add up. When he sits down to the books, the rest of us find somewhere else to be for a few hours.

"The shops are ridiculously busy, we need more men, Pres. We need you back."

"As soon as we take care of this asshole, I'll be back to work. Anything else I need to know?" The members all glanced at each other and shook their heads. "Good, I'll be back in the day after tomorrow. In the meantime, defer to VP."

Everyone stood, told the three of us to have a good trip, and left the clubhouse.

Nose, Slider, and I strode to our bikes parked out front and pulled on helmets. We fired up the engines and I led the way out of town.

We hit the highway ten minutes later. Being out on the open road was exhilarating. I lived to ride and feel free. It also gave me an opportunity to think about Callie. I knew by the way her eyes lit up every time she saw me that she was sporting a teenage crush. At least that's what I told myself because it couldn't be anything else. She was way too young for love.

Callie was a kid of eighteen, well almost, but that was beside the point. The point being, I was five years older, an adult, and had no interest in a relationship. So, why then, did I want so badly to see her happy, loved? It went beyond feeling sorry for her, being near her caused my body to react in ways I didn't understand. I found myself missing her when we're apart. The more time I spent with her, the more I wanted.

Oh yeah, what was that, *"you can move in with me,"* crap? Way to cramp your style—*idiot.* Not that I had anything to be cramped, I hadn't had a woman in months. The club girls just didn't appeal to me as much as they had in the past. Maybe I was becoming a fucking monk! As the bike ate up the miles, my mind warred with itself.

We reached the point where I'd picked up Callie and I pulled off to the side of the road. It was just on dark. Nose and Slider pulled alongside and we all removed our helmets.

"Pres?" Nose asked.

"This is where I found Callie, so he has to live around here somewhere. Callie said his property is heavily wooded from this side. It's too dark to search now, so I suggest we head to town and take a look around in the morning. There's a town ten minutes further up the road where we can get a meal and they have a hotel. Pretty seedy looking but it'll do for one night.

"Lead on," Nose said.

We pulled our helmets back on and hit the road.

***

Dinner at the small diner in Lidcombe was good—a stick to your ribs, homemade beef stew. The gravy was thick just like ma made it. The blonde who served us was a well-endowed young lady and spent the time making eyes at each of us in turn. She refilled our coffee mugs at the end of the meal and hung around making small talk. After a few minutes, Slider decided he'd had enough of her ogling him and held up his left hand, displaying the gold band on his third finger.

"Married, honey."

Nose then held his left hand up and Slider and I burst into laughter. He wasn't wearing a ring—he wasn't married. Fuck, he didn't even have a girlfriend. The blonde wasn't to know that, but Nose didn't even have a fucking third finger on his left hand, so he couldn't wear a band if he wanted to. He was also missing an ear, a nipple and two toes. No, I didn't look at his feet, or his chest, he told us. Some thugs had wanted information from him, but Nose wasn't prepared to divulge any. He didn't have any to give, so it would have been kinda hard to tell them what he didn't know. After torturing him for four days, and cutting off various parts of his body, they got the message and he was dumped unconscious on a vacant block in Foster.

Picnic, I'll explain his nickname later, found him and brought him to the club. I had Doc treat him and we looked after him while he recovered. Once he was back on his feet, he explained he had nowhere to go and said he'd like to join the club. He was accepted, had been a loyal member for six years, and was invaluable for sniffing out drugs. He's in his thirties but looks closer to fifty with the numerous scars and wrinkles.

Getting back to the blonde—she fixed her attention firmly on me once convinced the other two were unavailable. I wasn't going to spoil what seemed to be the theme for the night and tell the truth, so I held up both hands, leaned against the padded rear of the booth seat and said, "sorry, honey, I'm gay."

Nose and Slider had just taken a gulp of coffee which erupted with force from their noses and mouths after hearing me say I was gay.

The blonde wasn't impressed with the mess on her table and pretty much saw us for who we were—assholes.

"You don't have to fucking lie, just say you're not interested.

The three of us spoke at once, "not interested." Did I say we're assholes?

The blonde spun around and stormed off. We left before we got someone else offside.

Chapter Eight

JAKE

It took us almost two hours to find Ray's property and ramshackle cabin. When we pulled our bikes to a stop, the scrawny, skinny, fucker appeared on the porch with a smile on his face.

I nodded to him. The three of us stepped off our bikes, kicked out the stands, removed our jackets, and after draping them over our seats, set our helmets on top. We didn't hurry, and from the corner of my eye, I noted Ray shuffling with nervousness. Good.

The three of us approached the porch lined up side by side, like the *Magnificent Seven* except there were only three of us. We stood tall and, what can I say? I liked the analogy.

"Can I help you men?" Ray's voice shook slightly, further confirming his nervous state. He descended the steps and approached us with his chest stuck out like a fucking gorilla threatening others to stay away from his mate. Big mistake!

Slider and Nose were close enough to step forward and each grabbed one of his arms. The fucker started to struggle and kick out. So, my men kneecapped him and he dropped to the ground like a sack of potatoes. I must mention, my men didn’t let go of his arms, so the sudden drop ripped both shoulders from their sockets. He roared in pain, which didn’t bother us, we were in the middle of nowhere. No-one was gonna hear him. Once his shouting turned to whimpers, I stepped closer. A mixture of fear, anger, and pain shone from his eyes.

"What the fuck do you assholes want? I haven't done anything. I'll be having you charged with assault."

I moved even closer, hands fisted at my sides, itching to rearrange his pock marked face. "Do you know Callie McKenzie?"

His eyes widened and both eyebrows shot up to his hairline. "Where is the bitch? She's in for one hell of a beating when I get hold of her, she'll be sorry she left."

I was overcome with anger and rage with the way he spoke about my sweet Callie. My closed fist hit him in the solar plexus with the force of a battering ram and I heard ribs crack. He shouted in pain. I ignored him and dealt the other side a blow. An even louder crack sounded and he screamed. The more he slumped in my men's hold, the more pressure he exerted on his shoulders. He was in a world of pain, but it wasn't enough. I rained punches to his face, breaking his cheekbones, nose, cheeks, teeth, and probably his eye sockets.

I grabbed a fistful of hair and wrenched his sagging, bleeding head backward. "If you *ever* come near Callie again, I'll kill you. Consider this a warning."

I nodded to the men who twisted his forearms, I heard the crunch as the bones broke and dropped him to the ground. I stood over the bleeding mess and spat on him. Slider and Nose followed suit, before Slider aimed a well-placed kick to Ray's already broken ribs. We left him writhing on the ground and screaming in agony, dressed in our cuts, pulled on helmets, and rode away.

Did we care if the asshole died out in the middle of nowhere? Nope. When he'd threatened to beat Callie again, my no kill attitude took a leave of absence.

I rode away hoping the fucker would die and rot in Hell!

***

CALLIE

The next two days passed like time had flipped a switch and shifted into slow motion mode. Maree and the girls fussed over me, refusing to allow me to do anything. I felt guilty not doing something to help earn my keep. It was nice though, lying on the couch on the porch, dozing in the warmth of the sun. I was becoming stronger and my appetite had returned. The bruises were fading, my eyes were bright, and my hair was shiny again. What a difference ten days had made.

I was reading a book by my favorite author, enjoying the last of the day's sunshine when a familiar rumble caught my attention and shivers danced down my spine.

As Jake rode up on his bike, I stood on the porch and watched him climb off. As he strode toward me, he took off his helmet. His smile as he mounted the steps lit up my world. I was shocked when he gathered me to him and kissed my forehead. Fireworks exploded and I became light-headed. Thank fuck he had hold of me.

He whispered in my ear. "He's done with, he won't *ever* come near you again."

I gazed up into his gorgeous chocolate eyes. "Is he dead?"

"We didn't kill him, but we left him in a bad way." Jake released me, gathered my hand, and led me inside.

We stopped in the hallway while Jake removed his jacket and boots. I was on the brink of drooling at the sight of his muscles in a tight black t-shirt and I was sure my panties became wet. The man was drop dead, fucking gorgeous.

"Are you okay?"

No. "Umm, yes."

Jake laughed. "I meant about Ray."

"Oh, yeah. I honestly don't give a fuck whether he lives or dies. I just want him away from me and out of my life."

I followed Jake through to the kitchen.

"Uncle Jake!" Ella and Rosy threw themselves into his arms, and excited chatter, giggling, and kissing followed.

Mitch and Maree turned and smiled. It was obvious the girls' parents loved how their uncle was with them.

Jake placed them back on their feet, shook hands with his brother-in-law, and kissed his sister's cheek.

"How was the trip?" Mitch asked as Maree moved to the other side of the kitchen and switched on the kettle to make tea.

The rest of us sat down at the table. Rosy climbed onto Jake's lap while Ella climbed onto her fathers.

"Got the job done, but managed to upset one of the locals in the town where we stayed, so won't be going back there for a while."

"You were in town for one night and managed to upset someone? I swear, I can't let you out of my sight for two seconds. What did you do this time?" Maree removed a pot of tea from a tray and set it onto the table followed by four mugs, cream, and sugar. A glass of apple juice was placed in front of each little girl. Mitch and Jake grabbed for a cookie from a platter before it even reached the table and Maree slapped her husband's hand. His mock protest had us all laughing, and she gave him a hug before joining us at the table. "Well?"

We all crunched on the delicious cookies while Jake told us what I figured was the child friendly version of his encounter with a blonde waitress. I felt insanely jealous, but why? Jake had no interest in someone like me and I certainly had no claim on him. He could see other women if he chose. That was the key word in my dilemma—Jake was a man who dated *women*.

"Are you staying for supper, little brother?" Maree asked.

I held my breath willing him to say yes. I must be into fucking torture. The more he was around, the more I wanted him, and it was breaking my heart, piece by fucking piece.

I wouldn't mind staying for a couple of days if it's okay."

My heart performed a perfect Irish jig.

"You know you're welcome here anytime, I wish you'd stay more often. It makes mom happy when she knows you've had a decent meal and are being taken care of." Maree smiled and winked at me. "I guess you want to keep an eye on your girl, huh?"

I could have murdered Maree for embarrassing me. I felt my face heat and dropped my eyes in shyness when Jake turned my way.

"She's certainly looking a whole lot better than she did a week ago. Such a pretty face."

"I reckon Callie's beautiful." Rosy spoke around a mouthful of cookie.

"Yep, me too," Ella agreed.

I was hot before, now I felt like I'd been dropped into the middle of a fucking volcano! Beads of sweat formed on my top lip and I wiped them away with a napkin. When I glanced back up, Jake appeared to be studying me closely.

"I reckon you girls are right, she is a beautiful woman."

Fuck...I was trembling all over. Jake thought I was a beautiful woman?

***

After supper I watched Jake grab a beer and can of soda from the fridge. He invited me to sit out on the porch and I followed him out. My heart was hammering in my chest. I sat on the couch, he pulled a small table in front of us, and placed our drinks down. He sat and turned side on, his back against the arm of the couch, one leg folded under the other.

"Tell me about the club, Jake."

"We have about sixty members aged from twenty-one through to fifty-six. They all work jobs during the day and we meet up and hang out at the clubhouse of an evening. Not everyone comes every night but we all get together on weekends and ride. I own two workshops independent of the club but members work them. Ratchet is the manager for both. I work as a mechanic between the two, wherever I'm needed. They're on opposite sides of town and when one is quiet, the other is busy, or they can both be quiet or busy. We're flexible and put manpower where it's needed the most. Psycho does the books for the shops and the club business. Slider,

Viking Dave, Picnic and Joker are all mechanics. Nose and Construct are auto electricians. Doc Ink manages the club's tattoo parlor."

"Love the names, does everyone get one when they join the club?"

"Most already have them, especially the older ones. Those who don't, like our new prospects, we watch for a few days before giving them one."

He explained everyone's names, I especially loved Picnic. His nickname was given to him by the club because when they were on the road, he took care of the food. Joker's was obvious, and I knew from talking to him at the hospital, he loved to play pranks on the other men. He'd made me laugh when he told me stories of how he'd caught the other men out. "You missed, Construct?"

"Construct has a Doctorate of Engineering. He used to work on big building projects around Foster but grew tired of red tape and the lack of architectural imagination. After he joined the club, about eight years ago, he found out we needed an auto electrician. He did the course under Nose's guidance and loves what he does now."

"How long have you owned the shops, I mean you're very young for so much responsibility?"

"I've had them for three years... since I was twenty. When dad retired I was elected President and he signed the shops over to me."

"He obviously loves and trusts you." How nice it must be to be cared about.

"He does and I love and respect him. I call him when I need a second opinion on anything."

"What other business is the club in?"

"You ask a lot of questions."

"Sorry."

Jake patted my hand. "No need to be sorry. The club owns a housing construction business, about twenty of the men work in it and Construct acts as fail safe for any engineering issues that arise. Psycho is in charge of the books, and he has four other accountants to help him. The club also does as much for charity and the town as we can. In general, we're clean and stay out of trouble."

He looked worried about something. "What's bothering you?"

"We have a rogue member in another club who wants to infringe on our territory. Whoever it is isn't happy with an agreement I've come to with his President."

"Do you think he'll cause trouble?"

"I *know* he will."

"Hmm. So, Sally was a club girl before she married Slider? What happens if anything happens to him? Does she go back to being a club girl?"

"Yep, she'll become the property of the other members if something happens to Slider."

"Oh."

"Do you have plans for tomorrow?"

As if I would. "No, of course not. I'm still too weak to walk very far, and with my plastered arm, I couldn't drive even if I knew how."

"Are you up for a car ride?"

With you?

Do wild bears piss in the forest?

Oh yeah, take me wherever you like—heaven sounds good.

"Yes, of course. What did you have in mind?"

I know what I have in mind.

Callie, stop it!

Kid...Woman, remember?

But, he did say you were a beautiful woman.

Focus, girl. Focus.

"Not far out of town is a reservoir, the town water supply. Before you reach the main picnic area, a dirt track runs off to the left and leads down to a small cove. It's very private, great for skinny-dipping and a picnic. I'd like to take you out there for a few hours."

Put tongue back in mouth.

Eyes back in head.

Focus, Callie. Focus.

Wow, visions of Jake naked were sending my mind into hyperdrive. My heart was thumping loudly, it's a wonder he couldn't hear it. Imaginary hand shoots up in air and I scream out—*"take me."* Speaking calmly —"I'd love to go out there with you."

Jake popped the top off the soda and handed it to me. I thanked him and sipped while he unscrewed the top off his beer and gulped it down.

"Tell me about you, Callie. All I know about is your time with Ray."

"Not much to tell. Mama was a drug addict who preferred a hit to looking after me. She worked part-time in a bar downtown and turned tricks to feed her addiction. Now and again she'd come back to our apartment and toss a few dollars at me so I could eat. I stole my clothes from the Goodwill bin. As I got older, I stole food to feed myself and clothes from department stores. I have no idea who my daddy was, she said he was someone passing through town who exchanged drugs for her pussy. Legally my name is Callie Williams but when I lived with the McKenzie family, I started using their name. They made me happy for the first time in my life. I was at a good school, had nice clothes, and plenty to eat. It didn't last long—nothing in my life ever does."

"Why were you taken from your mama and out with Ray?"

"Mama got caught in a shoot-out between two gangs in the bar she was working. The police found out about me from one of the regulars and contacted child protection. They shoved me into a foster home where I was their slave and babysitter until they found someone who wanted to adopt me—Mr. and Mrs. McKenzie."

"You really have been surrounded by shit people for most of your life, haven't you?"

"Except for mother, daddy, granny, and now you, and your family, I sure have."

"I'm sorry, sweetheart."

I shrugged. "It's not your fault, I just got dealt a crappy hand."

Jake nodded, finished his beer and stood. "I'm tired, it's been a long couple of days. Let me take you inside before I go to bed."

I set the soda on the table, but before I could stand, I found myself swept into Jake's arms and against his hard chest. Damn, the man was turning me inside out. He carried me through to the bedroom and sat me on the bed. I gazed up at him.

"I'll get Maree to help you change for bed."

You can stay and help, I'm more than happy to let you.

"Get a good night's sleep and I'll see you in the morning."

Sigh, I'd get a better sleep if you stay here with me.

Get a fucking grip, Callie.

His plump, delectable lips grazed my forehead in a kiss and I sighed.

He chuckled and left the room.

Chapter Nine

CALLIE

I didn't sleep much, too busy fantasizing about Jake and what I'd like him to do to my body. Like it had any chance of happening, but hey, a girl could dream.

It was my eighteenth birthday, but I hadn't mentioned it to anyone, I didn't want a fuss. Being with Jake at the reservoir was more than enough.

The minute the sunlight filtered through the break in the curtains, I gave up on the idea of sleeping and left the bed. Wearing only a nightgown, I hurriedly padded down the hallway to the bathroom. I couldn't wait to take a bath, dress, and see Jake.

I hurried to the bathroom, and totally oblivious to the sound of the shower running, I burst through the door. My feet immediately froze to the tiled floor.

Jake was naked in the glass shower stall where he stood facing the door and washing his shoulder length hair. I took a few moments to drool over his body. I tell you no lie, the man was exceptional with muscles on his muscles. They rippled as he massaged the lather into his scalp.

My eyes drifted further south and....oh, my! The man's cock was rather large like the rest of him. Long, and oh, so thick. I might be innocent, but I was human. This was definitely the man I wanted in my bed as I completed the journey to womanhood.

As I stood worshipping him, his cock twitched and thickened. I finally came to my senses, and ordering my feet to get with the program and move, slowly backed toward the door. I was feeling thankful he hadn't seen or heard me. I'd almost made my escape when he spoke.

"Close the door on your way out."

Fuck! I took off like a startled gazelle being pursued by a lion. After slamming the door, I sprinted down the hallway to my room. His laughter echoed behind me. Once in my room, I threw myself onto the bed and pulled a pillow over my head. My entire body burned with embarrassment.

A short time later, a knock sounded, and I sat up to find Jake in the doorway with a towel wrapped around his waist. I swallowed hard at the sight of his bare chest. As a grin spread over his face, I wanted the floor to open up and swallow me.

"Bathroom's free. Oh, and lock the door." He walked away laughing.

I groaned, how was I going to face him again?

***

Breakfast was a tense affair for me. I was sure I spent the entire time doing a fantastic imitation of a lobster. The heat in my face was off the charts. Fortunately, the girls kept Jake distracted by telling him about school and their latest computer game conquests. It seemed their whole world revolved around their uncle when he visited. I, on the other hand, pretended fascination with my cereal.

When Jake spoke my name, I was startled and the table wore the tea I'd had in my hand. I jumped up before it could soak into the shorts I was wearing. Maree dashed for a cloth and while I apologized for making a mess, she soaked up the spill.

I glanced over at Jake to find a smirk on his lips and a twinkle in his eye. Fuck he unnerved me. Before he could say anything, his cell rang, and he answered. It gave me a few moments to compose myself.

There was silence as whoever was at the other end of the phone spoke.

"Okay, thanks for the call." Jake placed his cell on the table, relaxed back into his chair, and crossed his arms over his chest. The look he gave me had me wanting to crawl under the table.

Jake—One

Composure—Fled the state.

His eyes narrowed as he stared at me. I didn't think he was angry, but I dropped my eyes to my lap, and found my fingers fascinating as they intertwined nervously. From the expression on his face, I guessed our day together was off. I was disappointed, but I'd had so many disappointments in my life, what was one more?

"Callie?" His voice was stern.

I reluctantly lifted my eyes. "Yes?"

"Is there something we should know?"

Fuck, what had I done? I searched my memory, but apart from the spilled tea, I couldn't come up with anything.

Maree, Mitch, and the girls stared at me, waiting for my response. I didn't have one.

"I don't think so, I can't remember anything I've done wrong. But, if I have, I'm so sorry. I'll leave if you can take me into town." A tear slid down my cheek. Nothing good in my life ever lasted, but why today?

Maree sprang from her chair, kneeled down, and hugged me. "Enough, Jake, she doesn't understand."

His next words came from beside me and I huddled closer to Maree for protection. I was shaking uncontrollably, but didn't know why. No-one here would hurt me, especially not Jake. Maree peeled me away and stood as Jake crouched in front of me. He gently wiped away the tears.

"I'm sorry, sweetheart, I didn't mean to upset you. I was playing with you. I wanted you to admit it's your birthday. Doc Windsor called to see how you were doing and said to wish you a happy birthday. He also wanted to make sure I hadn't forgotten. As if I could. You weren't going to say anything were you?"

I shook my head; all eyes were focused on me. "It's not important."

"It is to us," Maree exclaimed. "Girls."

Rosy and Ella jumped down from the table and ran from the kitchen. They returned moments later carrying colorful boxes with bright bows attached to the tops. They set them on the table before me and stood waiting eagerly for me to open them.

"These are all for me? How did you know it was my birthday?"

"You gave your birthdate to the nurse at the hospital, and because it was close, I made a note of it. Maree is making you a special supper."

"With cake!" Rosy shouted.

"And candles!" Ella yelled.

Jake laughed. "Yes, with cake and candles. I have a picnic lunch ready. I want your day to be really special after all you've been through." He smiled at Maree. "Thanks, Sis."

"Thank you." I trembled with excitement and happiness, the fear immediately gone.

"Open your presents." Rosy pushed a box closer. "This is from me."

I lifted the lid and removed a pretty lemon and white sundress, it was the nicest dress I'd owned since being with mother. I kissed Rosy's forehead. "Thank you, it's very pretty, I'll wear it to supper tonight."

Rosy clapped her hands and moved to lean against her mother's legs. Ella stepped into her vacated place and thrust another gift at me. "This is from me."

I dispensed with the lid and lifted out a lemon sweater with ¾ length sleeves. It was perfect to wear over the dress on cool evenings. I cradled it against my cheek. "It's so soft. Thank you, Ella." I kissed her forehead and she smiled.

There were two boxes remaining.

"Those are both from Mitch and I, honey."

The first one I opened held a pair of strappy lemon and white sandals, the second a white purse. Everything was beautiful, and special, and brought tears to my eyes. "Thank you so much for everything. This is only the second time I've received gifts for my birthday. It's all perfect and I'm grateful."

"Are you ready to go?" Jake asked.

"Yes, I'll put these away in the bedroom first." Jake hadn't given me a present, but I didn't expect one. Spending the day with me was the best present of all.

"The girls will put them away for you," Maree insisted.

I stood from the table, hugged and kissed everyone, and thanked them again while Jake grabbed a basket, blanket, and towels from the bench. His previous mention of *skinny-dipping* jumped into my mind and I felt my face heat.

"We'll be back in plenty of time for supper, Sis. Around four." Jake escorted me through the front door.

"Don't cross the line, Jake." Maree shouted.

He closed the door, glanced at me and shrugged. Damn, Maree. I know I'm young and

Jake shouldn't be touching me, but fuck, it's the 21st Century and I wanted him more than I'd ever wanted anything.

I slid into the car, he fastened the seatbelt, and grazed his lips over mine.

"Happy birthday, sweetheart."

The brief lip lock set nerve endings firing and I was becoming rather an expert at doing an Irish Jig in my mind.

Hmm, Jake may be a gentleman, and might not want to cross the line, but if I had anything to do with it, by the time we got back to Maree's, he'd have crossed the fucking line clear into the next county! I hoped.

***

Jake eased the car onto the highway and increased speed as he drove toward our destination. I couldn't have wished for a better day. The sun was shining and there wasn't a cloud in the sky. I glanced at Jake.

"Thank you for spending the day with me."

"I had it planned out which is why I'm not going into the shop until tomorrow. I want your day to be special and I can't wait to show you my secret cove."

My gut clenched at the thought he may have taken other women to the cove. How many?

Why should I care? "You didn't have to do anything."

"I know but I wanted to." He shot me a sideways glance. "Are you okay about this morning?"

I felt my face heat, this was becoming a fucking habit when Jake was around. I blew out a deep breath. If I wanted him to treat me like an adult, I needed to start acting like one.

"I've never seen a naked man before. Ray always wore shorts and a t-shirt. Oh, fucking hell, just wash my mind out with acid. What a revolting sight he would have been naked. I'll take you any day, you're so fucking sexy."

I slammed a hand over my mouth and closed my eyes while Jake roared with laughter.

"Good to know you don't need acid to get me out of your mind."

Jake was so incredibly understanding and patient with me. He never took offence at what I said, and unlike me, he didn't embarrass easily. He turned the car off the sealed road and onto a dirt track. It was narrow and bumpy—as I said, it was a dirt track. I understood why others didn't venture there.

We remained silent as the car bumped and bounced its way along the rutted track toward the cove. When the trees appeared to part, the track widened and the cove came into view. I gasped at the sheer beauty.

Before us was a small, white sandy beach enclosed between national park headlands. The water was crystal clear and as blue as the sky. The surface sparkled in the sunlight, it was as if the water had been scattered with diamonds.

Jake stopped the car, turned off the engine and hopped out. A moment later, he opened my door and offered his hand. I unfastened the seatbelt, slipped my hand into his and stepped out. He wrapped an arm around my waist and all hell broke loose with my body. Picture shooting stars, fireworks, hand grenades exploding. I had them all going off inside me. It was time to cut the crap. I'd gone past having a crush straight to falling in love. I was in deep shit if I couldn't bring Jake over to my side. I was in danger of being hurt much worse than any beating I'd ever had.

"Earth to Callie."

I shook my head and gazed up into Jake's eyes. Fuck the man was tall. If he'd stretched his arm out, I could have stood with the top of my head in his armpit. Not that I wanted to.

Jake laughed and I skidded back to the present. "Sorry, what did you say?"

"You were a million miles away, what were you thinking about?"

Think of something, quick.

"Um, I've never been to the beach before."

Jakes eyes widened. "Never?"

"No, never. The McKenzies probably would have taken me if I'd stayed with them."

"This isn't a real beach, it's a cove which is part of the reservoir. Once the cast is off your arm I'll take you to a real beach where you can listen to the waves crashing on the shore and seagulls squawking overhead."

"I'd love that, thank you."

"Wait here while I grab the basket, blanket, and towels."

I watched as he strode back to the car, admitting his sexy ass, kicked off my sandals, and headed to the water. The sand was warm and soft under my toes, it was a wonderful sensation. The water lapped gently at the edge, shallow, and I stepped in. It was almost as warm as a bath. I wriggled my toes in the sandy bottom and giggled as the water buried them.

I didn't hear Jake come up behind me and jumped when he wrapped his arms around me, resting his chin on the top of my head.

"I love it Jake. It's so blue, and warm, and sparkly. I could stay here forever." He laughed at my childish wonder but I didn't mind.

"See that small island over there?" He pointed off to our right.

"Yes."

"In Spring, dozens of species of birds go there to raise their young. It's safe from predators and gives the chicks a fighting chance."

I turned my head and gazed up at him. "I'd love to see that."

Sometimes, I take a canoe and paddle around the edges. I watch the birds and all kinds of other reptiles. I'll take you out one day."

I spun in his arms. "You will?"

He tapped my nose. "I certainly will."

Without giving it a second thought, I raised on tiptoe, wrapped my arm around the back of his neck, and drew his lips down onto mine.

Jake hesitated when my lips parted, but only for a moment. He pulled me tightly against him and plunged his tongue into my mouth. I'd never kissed a man before. Hell, I'd never kissed a boy before and I was amazed I seemed to know what to do. My tongue dueled with his. I moaned. He groaned. His hands roamed my back. Mine clutched at his ass. His cock hardened and pressed into my belly. In my mind, I danced that Irish Jig once again. I was thrilled to be having an effect on him. The kind of effect I'd been hoping for. When he released me, we were both breathless.

Jake stepped back and turned away from me. I watched as his fingers dragged through his hair. His muscles were tense, he was in turmoil.

Chapter Ten

CALLIE

My heart thundered in my chest. What the fuck had just happened? Sure, I'd wanted him to take me, make me a woman, but I hadn't expected to have the courage to initiate anything.

I watched as he walked up the beach, his feet sinking into the sand, leaving tracks. I didn't follow, sensing we both needed a moment to think about what we'd just done. I dropped onto the warm sand, knees pulled up against my chest and head lowered. Jake leaned against a sand dune and peered out over the water. Even from this distance I could see he was troubled. I closed my eyes, hoping I hadn't ruined the first good thing to come into my life in....well, forever.

A few moments later, I sensed his presence before he dropped down beside me. When I lifted my eyes to him, turmoil was clearly etched on his face.

"I'm sorry," I whispered.

Jake gathered my hand, our eyes connected. "Don't be, it's just...." He dragged his fingers through his unruly hair. "You're too young, Callie. I'm a man who takes his women hard. I don't do relationships—EVER. They might be for some men, but not me. You've already suffered so much in your life and I won't add to it. Friendship is all I can offer."

Fuck, I wanted so much more, but I nodded. Friendship was better than nothing.

Jake squeezed my hand and the lines of tension disappeared from his face. Sunlight hit his eyes and gold threads danced. "How about our picnic and I'll have a swim while you paddle?"

I forced a smile while my heart was breaking apart piece by piece. Together we laid out the blanket and unpacked the contents of the basket. Maree had packed Caesar salad, roast chicken which turned out to be mouth-watering, and strawberry shortcake. By the time I finished eating, I was full to the brim and flopped down onto the blanket, peering up at the sky. Not a cloud dared to mar the blue perfection, and small birds fluttered about.

Jake sprawled out beside me, propped up on one elbow. I turned my head when he spoke. "I'll be leaving Maree's after supper tonight. Work is piling up because of the time I've had off and there are a few club matters which need to be taken care of. You'll remain at Maree's until your cast is off and then I'll help you with a job. I'm going to have a word with Psycho."

"Why?"

"He could do with some more help. I'll ask him to teach you about managing the books. It would serve multiple purposes. You'll have a decent paying job and be getting an education. Psycho will be able to take time off without worrying and I'll be able to keep an eye on you. When you decide you've had enough, and want to move on, you shouldn't have trouble getting work elsewhere."

"Didn't you say Psycho has four people doing the club's books?"

"He does, but they do the individual business books and Psycho checks everything is in order. He takes care of the books for the club itself and we have had a lot of incoming from the businesses as well as outgoings. Everything is thriving which means money is changing hands a lot more and it all has to be correctly recorded. I'm sure he'd like you helping him out."

"Do you always help lost people you find on the street? Are you a true knight in shining armor?"

Jake laughed. "I don't think so, can't say my leather shines a whole lot. Seriously though, we don't find many people in need of our help, but when we do...yeah, we help. We do what we can."

"I'd like to work with Psycho if he agrees. Thank you."

"I'll discuss it with him and let you know."

We lay on the blanket, dozing on and off. My eyes snapped open when I heard Jake stir, and watched as he stood, his back to me. He peeled off his shirt and threw it to the ground, his jeans quickly followed. He stood above me wearing only tight boxer briefs. A chant of *"turn around"* set up in my head, but I had to admit, the view of his ass wasn't to be sneezed at. His arms stretched over his head, and as he bent from one side to the other, his back muscles rippled. My pussy clenched, nipples hardened.

When he turned to face me, my lip hit the ground. I'd only seen him with a steamy pane of glass between us, now I was seeing him in digital technicolor.

I shoved my tongue back in my mouth and swallowed hard. The man was fucking gorgeous. Every muscle was hard and defined, he was the perfect example of a man with a six pack. His tattoos were artistic perfection, winding up his arms and over his shoulders. The bulge in his briefs was heart-stopping.

"I'm headed out for a swim." Jake smirked down at me, the man knew the effect he was having.

I couldn't utter a word My tongue had returned to my mouth, but was too fucking numb to enable speech.

He winked, turned, and jogged to the water, my eyes riveted to the rise and fall of his ass. There was no fucking way I could live in this man's home and remain 'friends.'

***

JAKE

I felt her eyes burning into my ass as I jogged down to the water and dived under beneath the waves. The coolness helped settle my overheated skin. Normally I would have stripped down completely, but I was already in trouble with this girl and didn't want to make things even worse. How the fuck was I supposed to deal with an eighteen-year-old who had just kissed me with more passion than any woman before her? Even my fucking cock stood up and took notice.

I swam straight out for a while before turning to my right and heading for one of the headlands a couple of hundred yards away. My stroke was smooth and even as I glided through the water. It relaxed my tight muscles. I needed to get thoughts of Callie out of my head.

Admit it Prescott, you want to take her into your bed and fuck her into tomorrow.

Did I mention her age?

Eighteen, man. EIGHTEEN!

She's legal age to fuck and a virgin for fuck sake.

She does NOT need you circling her like a fucking bird of prey.

I know that, but did I mention she ***is*** *legal age?*

Back and forth I went between my conscience and the devil on my shoulder. One minute she was old enough to be fucked, the next she was an innocent child. It was like plucking petals from one of those fucking flowers, you know the ones—'She loves me, she loves me not?' Or, in my case—'She's too young, no she's not.'

Callie had me so tied up in knots, I couldn't fucking think straight. A few days away from her would settle me down. I reached the headland and turned to swim back to the other before going back to the beach.

I shook the water from my hair, and strode to where Callie lay, her eyes closed. Her skin had a pink tinge thanks to the sun beating down on her. After drying myself off, and wrapping the towel around my waist, I crouched down beside my sleeping beauty. I took a moment to study her face. The past ten days had made a huge difference. Her sunken cheeks were filling out, bruises had faded, and her skin was smooth and clear.

I reached out and brushed my fingertips down the side of her face. Her eyes fluttered open, glazed with the haze of sleep.

"You're getting burned, sweetheart, we need to get you out of the sun."

Callie nodded and I helped her to sit up. While she struggled to wake, I dressed back in my jeans and t-shirt. Holding my hand out, she slipped hers into the palm, so I could pull her onto her feet. When she stumbled and crashed against my chest, I wrapped my arms around her waist. Sparks zapped through me on a direct line to my cock which flinched. This girl had the ability to turn my life on its fucking head and she had no idea the effect she was having on my body.

I ran a hand down her back and over the rise of her luscious ass. Fuck. Again, my cock jumped in my jeans and I groaned.

"Callie." My voice sounded husky to my ears.

She tilted her head back and gazed up at me with those gorgeous sea blue, innocent eyes that melted my heart.

"Yes?"

Fuck! My lips crashed down onto hers, she tilted her head to one side, and I deepened the kiss. My heart slammed against my ribs and realization hit me with the force of a freight train. I wanted this woman more than I'd ever wanted anything. Visons of taking her into my bed and never letting her out flashed before my eyes. The fact she was young didn't mean a fucking thing anymore.

Callie's hand slipped under my shirt, and her nails scratched at my back while my hands gripped the globes of her ass. I drew her down to the blanket, onto our knees. When our lips parted, we both dropped back onto our haunches and sucked in lungfuls of air. When our eyes locked, my desire for Callie was mirrored in her gaze.

Despite how I was feeling, I had to man up. This was a woman who'd experienced the worst life could throw at her. I couldn't do it. I couldn't fuck her and leave her.

"Callie, sweetheart." My voice was barely a whisper. "I want to fuck you into next year, claim you as mine, but I'm not the right man for you."

"Why aren't you?"

The shake in her voice broke my heart. I stood and took a few steps away, dragging fingers through my damp hair. After taking a deep breath, I turned back to face Callie.

"I'm too old for you. I live in an unpredictable world where bikers clash. As President, I could be killed at any moment. Too much has happened to you, so much suffering. I can't...I won't, take you as my woman and place you in danger. We have to remain as only friends. I'll find you somewhere else to live, but you can still work at the club."

Tears welled in her eyes, she stood, and with trembling hands, began packing our picnic containers away. I knew I'd hurt her but it was for the best. I helped her pack everything away, gathered it up, and we remained silent as we headed to the car.

Chapter Eleven

CALLIE

Just over five weeks had passed since I spent time with Jake at the reservoir. Eight weeks since he'd picked me up in the middle of the night. He's visited a couple of times, but things seem strained between us, and he makes sure we don't spend time alone. My heart broke when the last time he visited was to tell me I'd be staying with Hotpants Sally and Slider. He'd been deadly serious when he'd said I wouldn't be moving in with him. That his place was no longer an option. I tried to console myself with the thought I would see him at the club every day, at least the job offer was going ahead.

Nose had picked me up from Maree's and after heaps of tears and promises that I would visit often, he'd taken me to the hospital, staying close by while the cast on my arm was removed. The doctor announced the break had healed well, thank goodness. He gave me daily exercises to strengthen the limb and said if I wasn't happy with progress, he'd recommend physical therapy.

Nose escorted me to the club and showed me a small room set up as an office. He placed my suitcase off to one side by the door.

"Psycho, I'll leave Callie with you."

Psycho nodded, and Nose left to go wherever he was needed next. I'd only met Psycho once before and he'd been very kind to me. He said having me would lift a huge weight off his shoulders. His real name was Patrick, but he insisted I call him Psycho like the other members at the club. It felt awkward but I agreed.

We got down to work immediately and I took what seemed like hundreds of notes. After four hours, Psycho said we'd done enough for one day and called a halt. He said he was pleased with how quickly I appeared to be learning the ropes. It felt so good to be praised by someone for the first time in my life. He led me back toward what he called the club social room. We'd been discussing what we would be covering the following day as we walked. I stopped in the doorway to the huge room where Psycho said the men and women gathered to relax.

I stood observing the scenes playing out before me. Two of the younger members sat cross-legged on the floor, a gigantic television screen before them and remote controls in their hands. I watched as they leaned from side to side, racing virtual cars against one another. The room was furnished with one, two, and three seater chairs along with numerous small tables which at present held glasses of liquid and bottles of beer.

Some members sat chatting, women painted toenails, and other couples made out.

When my eyes caught sight of Jake, my heart shattered. He sat in one of the single chairs, a blonde perched on his lap. He sipped from a beer bottle before placing kisses on her bare shoulder while she busied herself at the side of his neck.

Psycho's whistle caused everyone, including me, to almost jump from our skins, and the place became deadly quiet. All eyes turned to the doorway, most landed on me. When the blonde on Jake's lap turned, I sucked in a deep breath. I could never compete with beauty like hers. All the air seemed to be sucked out of the room, I began to sweat and became dizzy. I needed to get out of there. Psycho, unaware anything was wrong, started introductions but I couldn't stay.

"Excuse me," I muttered. My eyes collided with Jake's before I spun around and dashed from the clubhouse.

I burst through the door and gulped in huge breaths of air. The air was warm but to my over-heated skin it felt cool. My heartbreak had nausea welling from deep in my belly. I took off down the street at a fast jog. I needed to find Mother and Granny. I was sure they'd be happy to see me and take me in, give me a home. It would give me a chance to find a job, one where I didn't have to see women draped over Jake every day.

Footsteps pounded the pavement behind me, I realized I was being chased. My heart thumped in my chest as I sped up and ran as fast as my legs would carry me. It wasn't fast enough, and when arms wrapped around my waist, I screamed out in terror. No matter how much I kicked and screamed, I couldn't get free, and there was no-one around who could help me. Tears flooded my face as I struggled against my captor.

"Callie, calm down!" Jake's voice shocked me. I stopped struggling and he spun me around in his arms. I took a step back to steady myself. "Babe, I'm sorry, I didn't mean to scare you. I was worried when you took off from the club. Where were you going?"

I gazed up at the man of my dreams and my heart shattered all over again. "I'm going to find Mother. Hopefully, I can stay with her and Granny until I find a job. I can't come back to the club, Jake."

His eyes became hooded and I caught a flicker of pain. "We need to talk, Babe."

I wrenched from his hold. "Go back to your fuck, Jake, I won't bother you again. Please thank Sally and Slider for their offer, and tell them I won't be needing to stay." I managed to wriggle free of his hold and turned to start off down the road, tears cascading over my cheeks. Jake followed, grasped my arm and spun me around. Again! If he keeps it up, I'll be too fucking dizzy to go anywhere.

"Jake, please leave me alone."

"Callie, listen to me." Jake sucked in a deep breath. "Mother and Granny are gone. I made enquiries while you were still at Maree's after you gave me their address. They've gone to England."

I couldn't believe what I was hearing but why would Jake lie? "No, you must be wrong. Why would they go to England?"

"Sweetheart, they were both British. Your mother had married her husband when he was posted to England with the Army. Both her, and her mother moved here to live with Mac. The neighbor I spoke to said after Mac died, and you were taken away, Mrs. McKenzie had a breakdown. Her mother was concerned for her wellbeing and took her back to England to be with family."

I stepped closer to Jake and pounded my fists against his hard chest. "You're lying. They have to be there, Mother and Granny are the only people who care about me, I can't be all alone."

Jake gathered me close and held me while I cried into his chest.

"I have no-one to turn to, nowhere to go," I blubbered.

He ran his hand up and down my back in a soothing motion and kissed the top of my head. For the millionth time I wondered why Jake couldn't like me. Why he couldn't want me the way I wanted him.

***

JAKE

The expression on Callie's face when she saw Larissa on my lap almost broke me, I'd never seen anyone so devastated. When she fled from the club, I had no choice but to follow. I couldn't allow her to run off as upset as I knew she was. Larissa protested—loudly but, I didn't care.

For weeks I've tried everything to get Callie out of my head, but every time I visited my sister's home, and saw how she'd blossomed, I wanted her more and more.

When I'd turned up, and found her seated beside Mitch on the love seat on his front porch, I almost lost it. Their thighs touched where they sat side by side, and my first instinct was to storm to where she sat, throw her over my shoulder, take her home, and lock her in my bedroom. I wanted to fuck her until she couldn't see straight, I didn't want any other man near her.

MINE! Screamed in my head.

Fortunately, before I reacted, and did something I'd regret, I'd come to my senses. I mean, it was Mitch for fuck sake, my sister's husband. She was the love of his life and the center of his universe.

After the visit, I couldn't settle. I found myself wondering what Callie was doing. Was she with another man? I'd tried to make out with a couple of the club women, but couldn't get a rise out of my cock.

The only person who seemed to interest my dick was Callie. It was driving me crazy. She filled my every waking thought and invaded my dreams when I slept.

Callie was fucking gorgeous, and looked every bit the woman she had become. Gone was the beaten up skinny girl. She had totally captured my heart.

***

When I caught up with Callie on the street, and she said she was leaving, going to the McKenzies, my heart sank. My emotions were all over the place. I couldn't accept that she wanted to leave, that I wouldn't see her again.

Well, dickhead, seeing another woman on your lap, making out, would have broken her fucking heart.

You knew she had a fucking crush on you.

How the fuck did you expect her to react, asshole?

The heartbreak I saw in her eyes brought me to my fucking knees. I'd never been affected by anyone the way Callie affected me. And, then I had to break the news about her beloved mother and granny. It had added to her distress and she shook life a leaf while I held her as she cried into my chest. When she said she had nowhere to go, no-one to turn to, it was all over for me. I felt the weight of weeks of turmoil lift from my shoulders.

Placing fingers under her chin, I tilted her head back. Fuck, the woman was falling apart. She was crushed and I'd caused her distress. I brushed away her tears and asked her to open her eyes.

"Callie, sweetheart, look at me. Listen to me."

She hiccupped a few sobs before her eyes flickered open and she quieted.

"I can't fight this any longer. I'm taking you home. I'm gonna fuck you until you don't know which way is up, then I'll hold you in my arms while you sleep. You're coming to live with me, you're mine and fuck the consequences.

"But...."

"No buts. I've spent the past six weeks thinking about nothing but you. I'm tired of fighting whatever this is, Babe. I want you. I need you. If it's not what you want, tell me now, because once we start this, I won't let you go."

Callie gazed at me in wide-eyed innocence. "I want this. I want you."

I nodded and captured her mouth in a spine tingling kiss which sent tingles straight to my cock. Was I doing the right thing bringing her into my life at this time? At a time when my relationship with the Panthers was so unstable. Fuck it. With Callie by my side, everything would be fine. I'd be invincible.

Chapter Twelve

CALLIE

I was confused about how I felt as Jake and I headed back to the club, my hand firmly held in his. I was thrilled knowing I was going to be with him, that he'd claimed me as his, but scared to death of being fucked by such a big man. I mean, I'd seen his equipment. I was well aware of what he kept tucked away in his jeans. The muscles of my pussy clenched at the mere thought of his long, thick dick pushing inside me. As happy as I was about being with the sexy biker, I also felt an overwhelming sadness knowing Mother and Granny were lost to me forever.

Jake squeezed my hand as we entered the club. He led me straight back to the social room where we came to a stop in the doorway, and I noticed nothing had changed since I'd run out. He released my hand, wrapped his arm around my waist and pulled me close into his side. A show of how possessive he must have been feeling. I draped an arm around his back.

"Bros, listen up," Jake shouted.

All heads turned our way and I felt my face heat with embarrassment. I hated being the focus of attention. My eyes scanned the room and I didn't miss the glare Larissa was sending my way. Fuck, if looks could kill, I would have been lying on a slab in the morgue.

When everyone quieted, Jake spoke. "Callie and I are officially an item and she'll be living with me as my woman. The President's woman. I expect her to be treated with the same respect as you do me. From tomorrow you'll see her around the club most days. She'll be helping Psycho do the books."

"Hopefully he'll be a little less fucking psycho," Slider called out.

While the members erupted in laughter, I saw Psycho scowl. "Remember who pays you, Slider. I'd be careful about getting me offside."

The expression on Slider's face was priceless as he mumbled an apology.

"Joking aside, remember what I've said. When I'm not here, take care of my woman, but keep your hands to yourselves, unless you want someone else wiping your ass for the rest of your life."

I glanced up and frowned at Jake not having a clue what he meant. When he caught me looking, he smiled and leaned down to whisper in my ear.

"If they touch you, I'll cut both their fucking hands off."

"Oh."

He turned back to the members. "I'm taking Callie home to get her settled in...."

"Fuck her you mean," Nose piped up and my face developed so much heat I began to sweat.

"Nose!" Jake cautioned before continuing. "I'll be back at nine tonight. Julio is coming in and I want all members here for a meeting. Take care of it VP." Viking Dave nodded to Jake.

"I'll start making calls now, everyone will be here," Viking assured.

Jake led me from the room, grabbing my suitcase before we stepped out onto the street.

"We'll walk. It's not far, but it would be awkward for you being on the bike and holding the suitcase. Tomorrow we'll get you a helmet, gloves, jacket, and boots. You'll be spending a lot of time on the back of my bike."

I nodded, although I wasn't sure about being on the motorbike again.

***

Jake's place was a two-story townhome in a gated community. The gardens were well maintained, and several people nodded our way, or called out a greeting as we passed. He unlocked the door, threw it open, and allowed me to step inside first.

I entered into a small foyer where a coat rack stood off to one side. Jake removed his jacket and boots and left the suitcase by the wall. He then took me by the hand and led me further inside.

The foyer opened into a large sunlit room. To the left was a state of the art kitchen which overlooked a small back garden.

"Do you cook?" I ran my fingertips over the black marble countertop while studying the appliances. Two large ovens with a six-burner stove top, a microwave, built-in coffee maker, and the largest fridge I'd ever seen.

Jake's booming laugh had me turning to face him. "Sweetheart, if I cooked I'd end up in hospital with food poisoning, and I hate to think what the men at the club would say if they found out I strapped on an apron and made a meal."

"Oh."

"I have all my meals at the clubhouse. Molly's our cook over there. What about you?"

"I can cook, nothing fancy. Basic stuff. Been doing it since I was about five years old. I'd have starved to death if I'd waited for mom to make a meal. I'd love to get some cookbooks and experiment. I'd like to cook for you."

"Sounds good to me, I'd like to eat breakfast and supper alone with my beautiful lady. Hmmm."

"What?"

"I was picturing you wearing nothing but an apron, your back to me." Jake wiggled his eyebrows and my face burned with heat. "Come on, I'll show you upstairs."

He gripped my hand and led me toward the staircase. I noted the glass topped dining table with six black chairs, a matching buffet stood against the wall. The living area had a comfy looking black lounge, and a gigantic flat-screen television was mounted on the wall above a sleek gloss cabinet. The floors were wooden, polished to a mirror finish.

I mounted the steps behind Jake and joined him on a small landing at the top.

"There are three bedrooms and two bathrooms up here, you can explore more while I'm out later. Right now, I want your gorgeous body in my bed so I can take your innocence.

I inhaled sharply, hoping I wasn't going to regret what I knew we were about to do. Jake led me to a doorway off to the left and flung the door open. I stepped over the threshold, my eyes gravitating to the largest bed I'd ever seen. I guess with Jake being such a big man, the size made sense. The frame was polished wood as were the nightstands on both sides. The bedding was a soft blue and white, the lamps at the side were chrome and glass. It was a modern, sleek bedroom but full of warmth.

Jake indicated two white gloss doors on one wall. "Closet and bathroom. There's a jacuzzi in the bathroom and believe me when I say we'll be trying it out later."

I felt the heat of a blush creep over my cheeks. "You have a beautiful home, Jake."

"I have a woman—Mavis, who comes in every day. I'm naturally tidy thanks to mom. She used to holler at us to pick things up, and put them away, saying if she'd wanted piglets she'd have bought a pig. Anything we left lying around was thrown out or given away. Maree and I learned real fast to pick up after ourselves."

"Your women must have loved coming here. I'm surprised you don't have a girlfriend or wife."

"Nope, happy to be single. You're the first I've brought here."

"I am?"

"Yep, I vowed I would never bring a one-night stand, or someone I didn't really care about into my home." He tapped my nose. "So, you're the first. I have no intention of this being a one-time only fling so, if that's all you're looking for tell me now."

"No, I think I want more. It may not be marriage and kids, but more than a once only deal."

Jake nodded. "Enough talking. I want you naked and in my bed."

***

JAKE

I stood Callie beside the bed and skimmed my eyes over her body. Eight weeks of healthy eating had done wonders. She'd blossomed, filled out in all the right places, and developed small breasts. I couldn't wait to see her naked. Her face turned a dark shade of red with my perusal. She was the untouched virgin, but I was the one who was nervous as fuck.

I stepped closer into her personal space, bent at the knees, and with one hand at the back of her head, I lowered my mouth over hers. Our kiss was gentle at first, lips mashing, tongues dueling. As our passion increased, teeth clashed and tongues fought for supremacy. My woman had a feisty streak and I suspected she could be bad in the bedroom.

My cock was rigid, aching with want, but come hell or high water, I was going to take this slow. I didn't want to scare her, but fuck, slow was near on killing me. This was new territory for me. Other women were happy to be pushed up against a wall where we'd fuck and then walk away. Callie was different in so many ways, she deserved gentle. Fuck, she deserved someone better than me, but she was mine and no-one else would touch her again.

I broke from her hold, and drew the shirt over her head to reveal a black lacy bra. Maree had done well when she took my woman shopping., I'd have to remember to thank her. I fingered the lace and felt her excited nipples poking at the flimsy material. Callie stood as stiff and still as a mannequin.

"Relax, beautiful. I won't do anything you don't want. You tell me no and I'll back away." She nodded and I zeroed in on the side of her neck, nipping at the soft skin. She smelled of roses, my favorite flower. Goosebumps prickled her skin as I ran my hands down her arms.

When she let out a soft moan I wanted to throw her on the bed and fuck her senseless, but I remained calm. I wanted her first time to be memorable. *Good* memorable.

My mouth found her already kiss swollen lips while my hands moved to her back and flipped the hooks on her bra. She flinched slightly when I drew the scrap of lace away, flung it to the floor, and covered her breasts with my hands. She was small, less than a handful but to me—perfection. I locked eyes with hers and watched as another blush crept up from her neck. Fuck she was gorgeous.

I stepped back and held her arms out to the sides, studied each perfect mound and rose-colored, pebbled nipple. She was bright red and I smiled.

"Fucking perfection."

I eased her back until her knees hit the side of the bed and sat her down. I gazed into her eyes while removing sandals from her feet. A quick brush of lips and I stood her back up. She watched as I plucked open the button of her jeans and slid the zipper down to reveal black lacy panties. Fuck me. The next time I visited my sister I'd be taking flowers and chocolates.

I pulled the jeans down Callie's slender legs and noted a few hairs from her dark thatch poking through the holes of the lace. She stepped from the denims and I flung them across the room. When I lifted my eyes back to hers, I saw cautious desire. Her skin was still flushed, she was unsure of herself and my attention.

"Fucking gorgeous," I muttered.

I gathered her in my arms and kissed her deeply, hoping to relieve some of her nervousness. My hands slipped over her ass, I drew the lace into her crack and filled my hands with her plump cheeks.

Callie was the first to step back this time, and for a moment I thought she was going to do a runner. Instead, she shocked the fuck out of me when she made quick work of my belt, the button, and zipper of my jeans, and slid her soft hand inside my boxer briefs. When she palmed my cock, I let out a loud groan. She jumped and pulled her hand back.

"Sorry."

Sheer panic was reflected in her eyes. I gathered her in my arms and held her tight. "Babe, don't be sorry. I've been waiting six weeks to feel your fingers wrapped around my cock and it felt a hundred times better than I'd imagined."

Gazing up at me and smiling, she slid her hand back into my briefs. I swear my dick cried out, hallelujah! I made short work of her panties and while the fingers of one hand pushed through her folds into the soft heat, my other hand tormented her nipples.

Callie was hot and wet, but nowhere near ready to take me inside her.

After brushing my lips over her nipples, I scooped her into my arms, flung back the duvet, and lay her down on the sheet covered mattress. All the while her hand stayed wrapped around my cock which leaked like a faulty faucet. I took only a moment to appreciate her body, my cock was screaming with want. I disposed of my jeans and briefs in one smooth move and chuckled when Callie's eyes widened.

Chapter Thirteen

CALLIE

Fuck me! I'd seen the man naked in the shower and he was big when he was soft. Hard, his cock was fucking enormous! I felt my eyes widen and Jake chuckled before he crawled toward me from the bottom of the bed. He kissed up the length of one leg, swiped his tongue across my pussy, dropped back to the ankle of my other leg, and kissed his way back up to my groin.

Sitting back on his haunches, his eyes boring into mine, he sank his fingers inside. He brushed over a spot which had me rearing off the bed.

"Fuck, what was that?"

"That, sweetheart, is your clit. Mmm, it's swollen and juicy."

He continued working his fingers deep inside me, while massaging my clit relentlessly. I arched from the bed, my nails scraped at his thighs, and my body trembled with want. I moaned, pushing against Jake's fingers, needing more. Stars danced before my eyes as spasms assaulted me. It was a surreal experience. I felt like I'd stepped outside my body.

Jake played me slowly, like a finely tuned instrument, until the spasms subsided and my body quieted. Total blissful satisfaction washed over me. I sighed loudly. He captured my lips, kissing me until I fought for breath. Supporting himself on his muscle-bound arms, he gazed down, concern in his eyes.

"Are you sure this is what you want? I won't force you into anything you're not ready for."

I threaded my fingers in his thick silky hair and drew his head closer. "Yes, I'm ready. Absolutely ready. I want this and have no doubts at all. Fuck me Jake, make me your bad girl."

Jake nodded and visibly relaxed, the tension eased. He slipped a hand between us and I felt the thick weeping head of his cock press against my entrance. Despite myself, I stiffened.

"Relax, beautiful, I won't hurt you more than is necessary."

"I know." And, I did know with certainty that Jake would never hurt me.

He pushed inside, I felt him filling me, stretching me wide. I relaxed once I realized I was feeling no pain. Little by little, Jake eased deeper. I glanced up to find his eyes locked on my face. Seconds later he stopped and remained still.

"Jake?" I was confused.

"I'm about to push through, sweetheart. I remember Maree saying it hurt like a motherfucker when she was breached."

He must have noted the sudden fear I was feeling.

"I'm assured it only lasts a moment. I'll hold still after it's done. Let me know when you feel okay."

"Just stop talking, Jake, and fuck me. The less I know the better."

He chuckled softly before crashing his lips against mine. My hands gripped his hips, he pulled back and slammed forward.

I yelped into his mouth as burning pain seared my insides. Jake stilled but deepened our kiss, taking my mind off the quickly receding discomfort. I wriggled against him, the pain gone, replaced by a delicious feeling of fullness. I latched onto his ass and pulled him closer, forcing his cock deeper.

I was sure I'd died and gone to Heaven. The feelings coursing through me as he pushed in and pulled out were like nothing I'd ever experienced.

"More, Jake," I begged. I had no idea what 'more' I wanted but trusted my lover to know.

I wrapped my legs around his waist and lifted my hips to him. The head of his cock hit the edge of my cervix over and over. My nipples pebbled and ached with the hardness. Goosebumps peppered my skin as Jake pistoned into me...faster...harder. His hands rested at the side of my face and I turned to place kisses on his wrist.

Bright lights danced in my vision before colliding with stars as an orgasm detonated. My nails scraped at Jake's back, the muscles of my pussy clenched, and I screamed out his name as the orgasm hit me full force. I shuddered, trembled, and bucked, as Jake held me tightly in his arms.

"Fuck, Callie!"

Jake squeezed me tighter, his rhythm faltering. I felt wet warmth filling me as his own orgasm overtook him. Our kiss was almost desperate, we clung to each other, our moans filled the room. Then, we quietened except for our heavy breathing. Jake rolled over, taking me with him. He seemed unwilling to let me go. His hand roamed my back, mine slid over his chest.

"Fuck, Callie, you rock my world. I knew you'd be bad ass in bed."

I giggled, thinking I must have done something right. Jake kissed the top of my head, it was the last thing I remember before falling asleep.

***

JAKE

I carefully untangled myself from Callie's hold, not wanting to wake her and slid from the bed. I didn't want to leave her, I wanted to stay, hold her in my arms and never let go.

I wasn't lying when I'd said she rocked my world, I'd never come so fucking hard in my life. The way she'd clutched at me with such passion had been suspected, but unexpected. I'd been with women who had been sexually active for years, women who had nowhere near her level of desire. Was it because Callie was the woman meant for me? The woman I was destined to be with?

I continued wondering as I padded to the bathroom where I hurriedly showered. When I returned to the bedroom, Callie was snoring softly. She stayed that way as I dressed. When I sat on the bed to tug on my boots, she stirred and her eyes fluttered open.

"You're dressed, is it time for you to leave?" she asked.

"Yep. I'll be back as soon as I can, but I don't expect it to be much before midnight."

"Okay." Callie yawned and smiled up at me, her eyes heavy with sleep.

I stood, leaned over, and kissed her forehead. One last glance at my sleeping beauty and I left the room, reluctantly heading for the clubhouse.

***

The parking area at the clubhouse was littered with bikes when I rode in. I eased my bike into the space marked 'President,' switched off the motor, stepped off and removed my helmet. As I set it on the seat, Viking Dave strode over with Julio and his VP—Ratman. They'd been outside chatting when I rode up, waiting on me I assumed. I shook hands with them both and thanked them for coming.

Julio nodded. "We need to get this shit sorted, I don't want a war any more than you do. I don't know who to fucking trust."

I noted the glance which passed between the two men. It was common knowledge the Free Lords and Panthers had their differences, but dad had managed to keep the peace and our territories divided. This was the worst tension I had seen between members of the two clubs and quite a few Free Lords' were operating on an extremely short fuse. It wouldn't take much to push them over the edge. Julio had confided there were Panthers who were on a knife's edge. As he'd said, we needed to get this shit sorted.

"Come on in, the members are here." Viking Dave opened the door as he spoke and I led the way inside and through to the meeting room.

I glanced around and found everyone was present, all eyes focused on me. I wondered for a moment if I had a rogue within, but quickly dismissed the ridiculous notion. I had no reason to question their loyalty, every one of these men had stood by me when dad had left the club. I'd been elected unopposed.

I was aware Julio knew most of my men, but he hadn't been introduced formally. I ushered him and Ratman into the room.

"Julio, Ratman, you know my VP—Viking Dave." Julio nodded as quiet dropped over the room and my men waited. As I introduced them one at a time, they shook hands with the Panthers. "Slider—Sargent at Arms, Nose—Secretary, Psycho—Treasurer, Picnic—Road Captain, and our most senior members—Ratchet, Cutter, Doc Ink, Construct, and Pimp."

My men were surprisingly polite and took a seat at the table after shaking hands. I stood behind my chair at the head of the table, indicating the two vacant chairs on my left for Julio and Ratman. VP sat at the table to my right. The scraping of chairs and opening of bottles ceased and I spoke.

"We all know why we're here and why Julio and his VP have joined us. For the past few months, Panthers' guns have been turning up in our territory in Foster. Julio and I believe this is an attempt to set both clubs against each other and tension is at breaking point. Julio?"

"Thanks, Pres. There's no doubt the guns are ours, and like your President, I believe if guns are being brought in, so are drugs. We have no reason to believe someone in the Free Lords is helping members of our club but, we can't rule it out. I have my suspicions and we need your help to draw them out."

"How so?" Slider questioned.

I took over. "We want Ratchet to start bitching about the club."

"Me?" Ratchet all but shouted.

I held out my hands to calm him down. "I want it to be you because you're in the shop all day and can bitch to customers. Word is sure to get around town, and hopefully rogues in the Panthers will hear and approach you."

"What the fuck will I say? Why can't you use Doc Ink?" Ratchet obviously wasn't keen on co-operating.

"Doc doesn't have as many customers come through his shop, his reach would be limited. I want you to bitch about Slider being

Sargent. Complain you're better suited because you have more experience. Complain about the club refusing to do drugs and guns, say the shops would make ten times the amount they do now if they were used as cover for illegal activities. Say you're tired of working your job for peanuts when we have Foster at our fingertips."

"I get the picture. What else?" Ratchet snarled.

I glanced over at Julio, none of my men knew what I was about to say. "You're going to kill me."

My men bounced from their seats, sending them flying every which way, and yelled out "what?" at deafening levels.

"Sit down and I'll explain." I waited for the men to calm and take their seats.

"Julio and I believe if the traitors hear about Ratchet being fucking disgusted with me, they'll make themselves known to him." I turned to Ratchet. "If they contact you, I need you to get them thinking about killing me, getting me out of the way so Julio can move in."

"I don't like it Pres, too much could go wrong." Slider voiced his concern.

"Yeah, what if Callie gets caught up in it?" Psycho had grown fond of my woman.

"She won't, I want you to work out of the office at the shop downtown until this is done with."

Psycho nodded his agreement.

"I'll be staying here at the club. My not being at the shop will give Ratchet something else to complain about. I've organized a vest so when you come for me, aim at my chest and I'll be fine."

Ratchet nodded but I could see he was livid. I'd speak with him again later.

"I want Shovelhead, Dog, and Chains to see me first thing tomorrow, VP. They'll be with me around the clock. When Ratchet shoots me, one of them will pronounce me dead. Hopefully, any other member who happens to be around at the time will rush to my side. That will give Ratchet and the rogues a chance to fuck off back to Julio and tell him what's happened. One of our prospects will alert the cops to get over to Julio's. They'll stay out of sight, but within hearing, when the men brag about killing me."

Ratchet stood, flapping his arms around like a madman. "Hang on a fucking minute. If I do the shooting, I'll be fucking arrested."

I shook my head. "No, you won't. I've clued Dave and John in and they know the set-up. As far as they know it's a sting to stop two of Julio's men from murdering me, and taking over the Free

Lords. To protect Julio, we can't mention guns or drugs. It has to all be about getting the Free Lords Club." Dave and John were local cops who we took our problems to.

"What can they charge them with?" Nose asked.

"Conspiracy to commit murder, and it should get them a lengthy time behind bars. Julio will make sure they have drugs on them when they're arrested so they'll be charged for that too."

"I still don't like it, but if it stops an all-out war, I can see we don't have much of a choice." Ratchet said.

I stood and everyone else joined me. "I'm headed home until morning. Ratchet, I'll be with Callie for a few hours each night so keep that in mind. You need to hit me during the day when there are less members in the club. We can't risk someone going apeshit."

Ratchet mumbled something I couldn't quite hear as he stormed past me and out of the room. I felt for the man, he was one of my most loyal supporters. Many times, he'd come to my defense when other members were arguing with me. It would be hard for him to be an asshole behind my back, but honestly, he was the only one I trusted to pull it off. I fucking hoped like hell that nothing went wrong.

"Okay, I'm calling it a night and going home to my woman."

I shook hands with Julio and Ratman, and thanked them for coming before leaving the clubhouse and heading for my bike. I desperately needed a fuck with my lady.

Chapter Fourteen

CALLIE

I felt the bed move and opened my eyes to find Jake sitting on the bed. Slivers of moonlight streamed through the window and lit up his face. He sat gazing down on me. I smiled as he pushed the hairs from my face and leaned forward to brush his lips across mine.

I sounded as sleepy as I felt when I spoke. "What time is it?"

"One thirty in the morning."

"Come back to bed."

Jake stood, stripped, and climbed in beside me. He lay on his side, I turned to face him, and was gathered into his arms. Wide awake now, I slipped my hand between us and fisted his stiff cock. He moaned and I jerked back. Jake grabbed my wrist, his reaction lighting fast, and pushed my hand back to his dick. I slid my fingers up and down his velvety length and he flinched. I hesitated, but his hand covered mine, keeping me in place.

"Sweetheart, if I moan, groan, jerk, stiffen, cuss, it means what you are doing is making me feel fucking fantastic. I don't want you thinking you're doing something wrong."

I relaxed after he explained I wasn't doing something wrong and continued fondling his cock. His hips lifted in rhythm, pushing his length faster through my fingers. Feeling confident, I scooted downward, pushed Jake onto his back and flicked my tongue over the slit of his weeping head.

His hips jerked upward and it felt good knowing I was giving him pleasure.

"Fuck, Callie."

Sliding down the bed, I held the base of his cock with one hand, opened my mouth, and swallowed him down as far as I could. When he hit the back of my throat, and I gagged, he pulled back.

His fingers wrapped in my hair, hips lifted, and moans filled the air around us as I sucked. My tongue swept along his steel hard cock and my fingers fondled his balls. He swelled in my mouth, every nerve ending in my body sparked, wetness flooded my pussy.

I squeaked in surprise when Jake flipped me onto my back, and held himself over me, his cock resting at the entrance to my pussy. His eyes seemed to be searching mine, and he must have been satisfied with what he saw because his lips crashed against mine and his cock slammed deep inside.

Our fuck was frenzied, desperate. I clawed at his back, his ass. I wanted to climb inside his skin. The air around us crackled with arousal…need…want. Our lips parted and we both gasped for air. When the orgasm crashed into me with the force of an out of control freight train, I screamed his name into the air.

Moments later, his mouth covered mine and his cock pulsed as his hot seed spilled deep.

We lay side by side, still breathless, basking in the aftermath of our post orgasmic bliss.

I would never get enough of this man. I prayed to God, someone I had never believed in, to keep us together. To give me something good in my so far fucked up life.

Jake rolled away and sat up, fingers combing his hair. “Fuck.”

I guess God hadn't been listening. I jumped up to sit beside him. “What?”

“Condom, we haven't been using a fucking condom.”

“Shit. Well you know I'm clean, and I'm on the pill. Maree organized it for me with Doc.”

"I'm clean too, had my last test three months ago."

Jake breathed a sigh of relief and we lay back down, cuddled in his arms, I fell into a deep sleep.

***

Jake was raised on one elbow gazing down on me when I opened my eyes. Sunlight filtered into the room.

"How do you feel, beautiful?"

I stretched my arms over my head and let out a sigh of contentment. "Like I want to stay here for the rest of our lives."

He laughed softly. "Psycho wouldn't be happy if you don't show. He's been spouting off to anyone who'll listen about how fast you learn stuff. He said he doesn't know how such a beautiful and intelligent woman ended up with me."

I giggled. "Luckiest night of my life was when you stopped out on the highway."

Jake nodded, his eyes serious. His expression caused my gut to clench.

"We need to talk."

Hot tears sprang to my eyes. "I knew it. Fucking God can't give me one fucking break." I moved to leap from the bed.

Jake sat up, reached out, and dragged my naked body onto his lap. His boner pressed against my ass. "Whoa, I have no idea what the fuck you're thinking or where the fuck you think you're going."

"You were going to tell me you're not interested and want me to leave." My blubbering had Jake tilting my head so I was forced to look at him.

"Stop! Right fucking now! Listen to me!"

He looked mad, so I wiped the tears from my eyes, swallowed hard, and stayed quiet. My breath hitched on one last sob before I calmed.

"I'm only gonna say this one fucking time so you'd better be listening." I nodded as Jake scowled, his hands now at the side of my face. "I'm more interested in you than I've ever been in anyone. You're too young and too innocent, not meant for my world, but I can't, and don't want to, get you out of my mind. I need you. I feel different when you're with me. Happier, more settled. Maree is gonna go apeshit when she finds out I've had you in my bed but I don't fucking care. Right or wrong, you're mine now and you're going nowhere. Am I perfectly fucking clear?"

"Yes, but...."

Jake pressed his fingers to my lips. "There are no fucking buts. If I wasn't sure I wanted you in my life, I wouldn't have announced to the members that you're my woman."

"Okay." My heart was performing tumbles and flips worthy of an Olympic gymnast.

He kissed me gently. "What I wanted to tell you is, we have a problem with the Panther's MC from Corgette."

My gut clenched again. "Trouble?"

You know those tumbles and flips my heart was performing a moment ago? They've transferred to my belly and are being performed at twice the speed. I'm beginning to feel nauseous.

"It's nothing for you to worry your pretty little head over. We have issues in the club from time to time. Usually it's when someone's head gets too big and they have grand delusions about taking over. For the next couple of weeks, until we have this sorted, I've asked Psycho to work with you in the office of our shop downtown. I don't want you working in the clubhouse."

I stayed silent for a moment as semi-relief washed over me. "That's all?"

"That's all."

"I was scared for no reason?"

"Yes, you were."

I flung myself against my sexy man's rock-hard chest and peppered his face with kisses. After a moment, he sat me back on his thighs.

"As much as I'd like to fuck the ever-loving daylights out of you, Psycho will be here in just over an hour to give you a ride. Go and have a shower while I get dressed and we'll have breakfast."

One last peck on the lips and I was lifted onto the floor. I swayed my hips as I made my way to the bathroom and smiled when he let out a loud groan. "You're fucking bad, what have I unleashed?" I glanced back over my shoulder. Yep, he was checking out my ass.

***

Two Weeks Later

JAKE

The past two weeks, living with Callie had been the best of my life. I was falling for my bad girl. Hard. I wondered how I'd ever lived without her. I leaned back in my chair and folded my arms across my chest, forgetting about the emails I'd been answering.

Thoughts of my sexy Miss, who now some amazing ink thanks to Doc, filled my head. I pictured every soft curve, the gentle roll of her ass, a smile which lit up my world, a heart of gold, and fucking which was off the charts.

My lady had become very adventurous and it was only a matter of time before I claimed her ass. I would own every part of her then.

The other club members adored her, even the women who can sometimes be jealous of new blood, seemed to love her. But, she was mine. Did I say I was falling? Let me correct myself. I've fallen. Deep down I knew I was in love with my beautiful lady.

"Pres?" Slider interrupted my thoughts and I swiveled my chair to face him.

"Yep?"

"Just got word from Ratchet. He's on his way with Cheapskate and Big Bass."

I nodded and stood, showtime. "Chains and Dog?"

"They're in the living room playing a game of chess. It's was almost time for Chains to relieve Dog so it's good timing. It's only the four of us."

Ratchet was aware of picking this time of day for the job when there were never any women in the club and most members were at work.

"Good." I stand and strip everything off the top half of my body. Slider helps me on with the bullet proof vest before I tug my wifebeater and jacket back on. "I hope to fuck this all goes as planned. If anything goes wrong make sure you take care of Callie. She's not to become a club woman." The thought of her being a convenient fuck for the club members chilled my blood and I shuddered.

Slider slapped my back in reassurance. "It'll all be fine, nothing will go wrong. Ratchet is the best shot in the club, he won't let you down. I still wish we could have done something about those two pricks when we found out it was them running guns and drugs into Foster."

"We had no proof. It's Ratchet's word against theirs. It's not enough to satisfy the cops let alone some of Julio's members who have a short fuse where we're concerned."

We strode side by side to the living room, and as soon as Dog and Chains saw us they stood and approached. We gave each other a chin lift.

"Ready? They're on the way."

The young men nodded, but their expressions were wary, something flashed behind their eyes when they glanced quickly at Slider. I wondered what the fuck that was about but didn't have the time to ask. I turned to face Slider.

"If anything goes wrong, and I'm not around to do it, make sure they're patched over."

"You'll be here, Pres."

I nodded but couldn't get rid of the ominous feeling which had settled in the pit of my belly. Something didn't feel right. I glanced at my watch—2pm. They would arrive any minute. And, speak of the fucking garbage.

I turned to see Cheapskate and Big Bass standing on each side of Ratchet who was pointing a .38 at my chest. It seemed a bit high, and off to one side, his hand trembled slightly, but I trusted him, and hoped to fuck he was accurate.

"Well, well, well, if it's not the fucking gutless President himself. The fucking interfering asshole who's been trying to negotiate with the Panthers. Ratchet said you'd be pretty much alone at this time of day." Cheapskate spat.

From the corner of my eyes, I saw Chains and Dog move to my side. Slider stood back, watching as he'd been instructed.

I took a step forward. "Put the gun down, Ratchet, and we'll talk."

The men either side of him laughed.

Cheapskate seemed to be the more aggressive of the two and he stepped toward me. "There's been enough fucking talking to last a lifetime. Julio won't run drugs and guns into Foster while you're alive so we're gonna remedy the situation."

"Are you stupid? What about witnesses, are you gonna kill them too?"

Ratchet was tasked with convincing the Panther men that most of the club members would be glad to see the end of me.

Big Bass gave a chin lift toward my men. "You with us or this asshole?"

My three men moved behind him in a show of support, exactly as we'd discussed. Big Bass grinned at me, believing he was the victor.

"Looks like we don't have any witnesses, Pres." Ratchet grinned but I could see the nervousness in his eyes. "It's time we ditched your fucking morals and made us some easy money."

"We're done talking, get rid of him." Cheapskate snarled.

Ratchet took aim, but his hand had a visible shake, and I began to worry. A few seconds later I found out I had good reason to. The bullet pierced my shoulder and I roared in pain. Fuck, it burned like a motherfucker. I dropped to my knees before falling onto my back. When I clutched at the wound, warm sticky blood covered my hand and dripped through my fingers. Fuck, I was gonna fucking bleed to death. I glanced at Ratchet who had a look of terror in his eyes. I was scared to death he'd blow our plan and shook my head ever so slightly, warning him to do as we rehearsed.

Pain engulfed me, spots danced before my eyes.

Slider wrapped his fingers around my wrist while Chains had his at the side of my neck, they both looked worried sick.

"He's dead, you better get out of here. We'll meet you at the Panthers clubhouse after we take care of things here." Slider held out his hand. "Give me the gun and I'll get rid of it."

I watched through hooded eyes as Ratchet handed the gun over. I was flirting with darkness. The tingling in my arm had turned to numbness. I couldn't believe Ratchet had actually fucking shot me.

Ratchet raced from the clubhouse with the Panthers following. I couldn't hold my eyes open any longer. Moments before I sank into darkness, I heard a blood-curdling scream. Callie! Fuck, no! It was the last thing that crossed my mind before I blacked out.

Chapter Fifteen

CALLIE

Psycho needed to head to the bank, so since it was Friday, we decided to call it a day. I wanted to surprise Jake at the club, maybe we'd have supper at a nice restaurant in town before we headed home to our bed.

Home.

Our bed.

I'd given up on both before Jake came into my life. Actually, I'd stumbled into his.

I watched as Ratchet and two other men rode away and pushed open the clubhouse door. A smile was plastered on my face as I headed for the living area. I froze in the doorway. Jake was lying on the floor, Slider and Chains by his side. Blood was all over the hand held at his shoulder. Jake was as white as a ghost.

Chains was speaking, but I didn't hear, my eyes were glued to Jake's lifeless body. The words, *he's dead*, hung in the air and brought me out of my shocked state. I screamed hysterically before spinning around and dashing outside. I heard Slider shouting my name but didn't stop running.

Irate drivers honked their horns when I dashed blindly across the roads in front of them.

I ducked into a dark alley, breathless, my heart beating erratically, feeling overwhelmed with nausea. I shimmied in behind a couple of smelly dumpsters and lowered myself to the ground. Dropping my head into my hands, my chest heaved as I sobbed uncontrollably.

My heart was ripped to shreds. My world had imploded. Jake—the only man I had ever loved with everything I am, was gone. I wanted to leap from the top floor of a skyscraper, not wanting to go on without him. Trouble was, my fucking will to live was too strong. I was the ultimate coward. For what seemed an eternity, I cried harder than I'd ever cried.

Darkness was falling, and for about the thousandth fucking time in my life, I had no-one to turn to. I couldn't go back to the club for help—I was *their* woman now. I shuddered at the thought of having another man's cock shoved inside me.

I was Jake's and now he was gone, there would never be someone else. I couldn't return to the house. It was no longer home and would be the first place the club members would look. So, the streets it was.

I had a little money, two hundred dollars. Jake insisted I always have cash on me in case of an emergency, there hadn't been one until now. The money wouldn't go far, so I sat silently formulating a plan to get out of Foster. I was too big a target to stay here, so Corgette it was going to be. I had a better chance of not being found in the city. I dragged myself up, and keeping to the shadows of buildings, slunk to a gas station on the outskirts of town. When I heard bikes moving slowly along the streets, I ducked into dark doorways until they'd passed. They were men from the club, searching for their new fuck. Well, they weren't getting it.

My plan, as flimsy as it was, would take place at the gas station. I knew from what Psycho said that most people left the keys in their ignition when they went in to pay for gas. I would steal a vehicle, drive to Corgette, and leave it on the side of the road when I reached the city limits. I knew it was wrong but I had no other way to get the hell out of Dodge. A bus, or hitching a ride, would leave a trail for Jake's men to follow. At this point in my life, I no longer gave a flying fuck about what was right or wrong. I'd had so much shit thrown at me, I was done caring.

***

The biggest problem I had, the largest hole in my plan? I didn't have a fucking clue how to drive. I'd watched Psycho when he drove me to and from the office and it didn't look too hard. Somehow, I'd manage.

I stayed under cover of darkness while I scanned the vehicles stopped at the station. A small white car, off to one side, no-one nearby, caught my attention. I skirted around the rear of the station, and when I came up on the car, found it empty.

Hurriedly, I slipped behind the wheel and breathed a sigh of relief when I saw the keys dangling from the ignition. I turned the key and the engine came to life. Remembering what I'd seen Psycho do, I shifted into gear, released the handbrake and slammed my foot on the accelerator. The car shot forward, clipped a post and zig-zagged through the station out of control.

Way to not get attention, Callie!

"Fuck!" I wrestled with the wheel and eventually managed to direct the car onto the highway. According to the signposts, I was even headed in the right direction. How I wasn't killed was a mystery. I shot onto the road causing other vehicles to swerve. Horns honked as I sped down the road in anything but a straight line. I glanced down at the dashboard to see I was traveling at one hundred miles an hour. I couldn't see a fucking thing. Vehicles coming toward me flashed their lights even when I was on the right side of the road. It was then I realized, I hadn't turned on the headlights. I had no idea how to do it. I fiddled with one lever after another until the road before me lit up.

"Not so hard," I scoffed.

Once I was able to see where I was going, I concentrated on keeping the recalcitrant vehicle on my side of the road at all times. When I came up on a slower car, I checked nothing was coming toward me and sped past. I was getting the hang of driving and felt elated with the fact I'd managed to escape. It was to be short-lived.

As I hit the city limits of Corgette, lights flashed behind me, lighting up the rear-view mirror. I flattened my foot to the floor but the little car had no more to give. The cop hit the siren, but I kept going until another cop on a bike darted out of the bushes. There was no way I was about to kill anyone—especially a cop. I almost slammed the goddamn brake through the floor I hit it so hard. At the same time, I turned the wheel away from the cop and sent the car spinning in circles toward a huge oak tree. This was going to end badly. I held my breath, waiting for the sound of breaking glass and metal twisting but, it never came. The little car came to such an abrupt stop, I was flung sideways into the passenger seat. Cops swarmed the car. Okay, so it was only three cops but it seemed so many more at the time.

Someone yelled, "put your hands on your head."

I complied.

When the door was flung open and I gazed into the barrels of two guns, I wished they would shoot and put me out of my misery. Fortunately, or unfortunately, depending on your perspective, they didn't shoot. Instead, I was dragged from the car and read my rights while my hands were wrenched behind me and handcuffs slapped in place. I was in a shitload of trouble.

A cop held his hand on my head as he shoved me into the back seat of his car. He drove me to the police station in downtown Corgette where I was led into the building. After being fingerprinted, written up, and formally charged, I was thrown into a holding cell. Well, not thrown. Guided. But thrown sounds so much tougher.

Being a Friday night, I was told to settle in and get comfortable, I wouldn't be seeing court until Monday. The guard informed me I would have a court appointed Defense Lawyer for free. I thought that was pretty good because I had no money to pay for one. That's sarcasm by the way. The lawyer would meet with me at the courthouse before my case was called to be heard. I didn't have it in me to care. I'd lost everything. This bad girl of Jake's was well and truly broken.

***

The weekend passed at the speed of a fucking snail on crutches. I managed a few hours' sleep in between druggies, prostitutes, and other law-breaking women like me being tossed into the cell.

By Monday morning only three of us remained. One was in to sleep off an alcoholic binge from the previous night, she was in her mid-twenties and answered to Bella. The other woman was a seasoned prostitute who went by the name of Drucilla. And, I'd thought my real name was bad. She'd come in sometime around three in the morning and said her pimp would be in soon to post bail. Lucky her—maybe.

"Calliope Green!" a cop shouted. I'd had to use my legal name when I was booked. Who the fuck calls their kid, Calliope?

I stood and crossed to the door. "Yep."

"Court."

He opened the metal door, grabbed my wrists, and snapped cuffs into place. My hands were in front of me this time. I guess they'd figured out I wasn't much of a threat. I was manhandled through the station, taken outside, and shoved into a cop car. It turned out to be a short ride to the Court House. We could have walked, it would have been fucking faster considering the traffic.

Again, I was manhandled... No. Wait. To be fair, I have to concede, I wasn't treated roughly. Maybe, guided with a hand on my upper arm would be fairer. Anyway, I was taken to a small room where a tall thin man with a really skinny neck stood waiting.

"Davis, your client, Calliope Green." The cop led me to a chair and waited for me to sit before leaving the room.

"Young lady, you're in a world of trouble. My name is Davis as you heard and I'll be attempting to defend you."

"Mr. Davis, I don't give a flying fuck if they lock me up and throw away the key. I've been beaten to within an inch of my life, got no-one, lost everything, and I just don't fucking care what they do with me now."

"If you go before Judge Stanley with that attitude, you may end up in prison for a very long time. Give me something to help you, Calliope....."

"Callie," I snapped.

"*Callie,* you're charged with Grand Theft Auto, Speeding, Driving in a Reckless Manner, and Operating a Vehicle without a License. What were you thinking, why did you do it? Give me something to take to the Prosecutor, you're young, you have your whole life in front of you. Don't waste it in prison."

Davis was rather a nice man. I sighed loudly. "I'd just lost my boyfriend who'd meant the world to me and I needed to get out of town. I wasn't thinking clearly."

Davis raised his eyebrows so high they disappeared into his hairline. "This happened because you broke up with your boyfriend?"

Yep, that will do. No need for him to know my biker boyfriend was murdered and I knew who did it. Hmm, testimony against a biker gang would cause me a shitload of pain. Nope, break-up sounds good. I nodded just as the door opened and the cop informed us we were wanted in court.

Chapter Sixteen

CALLIE

I walked beside Davis who gave a me some last-minute instructions as we headed to the Courtroom. Once inside, the cuffs were removed and I sat as instructed. Davis crossed to the table beside us and conducted a whispered conversation with another man. He returned to our table when my case was called and I was asked to stand. I was instructed to approach the Judge where another man told me to place my hand on a bible and swear to tell the truth before God. I almost cracked up laughing. Yep, God has my respect. Not! Swearing to tell the truth with my hand wrapped around the man's dick would have had more meaning. I did it anyway to save prolonging things. Swore on the bible, not the man's dick.

I was led into the dock and the two lawyers sat. The Judge addressed me. He was soft-spoken and I liked him.

"Ms. Green, you're aware of the charges against you?"

"Yes, Your Honor." Good, huh? Davis told me to answer that way, it was one of the things he spoke about as we headed into the courtroom.

"How do you plead?"

"Guilty of all charges, Your Honor."

"Defense Lawyer?"

My lawyer jumped to his feet. "Davis, Your Honor."

"I know who you are, Davis. You're aware of the guilty plea?"

"Yes, Your Honor. We ask for minimum incarceration due to our client not being of clear mind when she stole the car and sped down the highway."

"Alcohol or drugs?" The judge sounded irritated now and glared at me before turning his attention back to Davis.

"Neither, Your Honor. The accused had recently broken up with her boyfriend. He was her first and she took it extremely hard. She had no family and no friends to turn to for help. We request a lenient sentence with consideration to the circumstances and her age. We don't believe it will happen again."

"Prosecution?"

The other lawyer pushed onto his feet. "Yes, Your Honor."

"Are you in agreement with the application for a lenient sentence?"

"Your Honor, I took the opportunity to speak with the Police involved in this matter and they informed me that Ms. Green could have crashed into a motorcycle officer during their pursuit and it would have been catastrophic. Instead, she swerved violently away from the officer, causing her car to spin out of control. This endangered her own life and indicated she had no intention of putting others in danger. The accused is barely eighteen years old. We feel she acted without thinking and has remorse for her actions. She has no criminal past and we believe a lenient sentence is warranted."

Ha, remorse? Not fucking likely. Well, maybe. Yeah, I guess I am sorry I stole a vehicle which someone must have worked hard for. And, yep, I am sorry I put other lives at risk. I'm not *all* bad.

The lawyers sat and I watched the Judge searching through a book. He must have found what he was looking for because he nodded, closed the book and peered over at me.

"Will the accused please stand."

I got to my feet as did Davis.

"Ms. Green, your actions on Friday night were irresponsible. You placed a lot of innocent people in danger—adults, children and officers of the law. Irresponsible, but not malicious I'll concede. I understand your emotional turmoil but I can't condone, or overlook the actions you took. Due to the favorable report from the Police Officers involved, and the prosecution, I have decided to sentence you to six months minimum security in the Women's Correctional Facility in Foster. I hope, young lady, that you learn from this and I won't ever see you back here."

"Thank you, Your Honor."

I was led from the dock, handcuffed, and escorted from the Courtroom. Davis joined me at the door.

"Callie, don't blow this."

"I won't and thank you."

We nodded to each other before a cop led me outside to his car, where he informed me I was to be taken back to the police station to wait for the bus which would take me to prison—my home for the next six months. Look on the bright side, I had somewhere to live and meals for the following six months.

***

The bus drove through a set of large metal gates, the only break I could see in the metal and barbed wire fence. The buildings were dull gray brick and bars graced the windows. We came to a stop on what appeared to be a parade ground. I peered through the window to see six guards standing nearby, four females and two males. About ten of us were herded from the vehicle and ordered to line up before the guards. As the bus drove away, the prison staff studied their new charges. A tall skinny guard who looked like she could do with a good meal spoke.

"Follow me."

She swiveled on her heels and the other guards ensured we did as we'd been told.

The room we were led into had a concrete floor, it was cold and unwelcoming. Suited a prison, I guess. I jumped when the metal door clanged shut and turned my head to see a guard turning a key in the lock. If I hadn't already realized my days of freedom were over, I knew it then. We were alone with only the female guards. My gut clenched, there had to be a reason why the male guards had left. I didn't like where my thoughts were headed. I'd been watching too many prison movies and my imagination ran wild.

We were lined up again before being led away, one by one. When my turn came, I was taken into another room with a shower against one wall. No curtain. No glass door. No privacy. The guard ordered me to strip. Nope, wasn't happening. She clipped me hard on the arm, and I sensed refusing would put me in a whole new world of pain, so I removed every stitch of clothing I had on.

I was instructed to stand with my legs spread wide and my arms held out at my sides. She proceeded to check every orifice. I had no idea what she was looking for so far up my ass and her probing hurt like a motherfucker. I welcomed the shower, and once clean, dressed in the jumpsuit she thrust at me.

The bitch then took me through to a woman who was introduced as the prison councilor. Mandatory, I was informed. There was no fucking way I was telling her anything so I spun a few stories she seemed to accept. For some reason I'd taken an instant dislike to the surly woman and was glad to get out of her office.

Next, I was introduced to the woman who would be my Peer Inmate. She would take me to my cell, teach me the rules and routines, and guide me throughout my incarceration. Her name was Mandy, and unlike the councilor, I felt an instant connection. She was in her late forties and explained she was in for running a red light and killing a pedestrian. Her sentence was six years. It seemed awfully light. Mandy explained she'd been convicted of Vehicular Manslaughter and yes, her sentence was light. She'd been rushing to pick her kids up from school and had driven through the light as it turned red. Unfortunately, a man aged in his late eighties had chosen to cross the road at the same time, also on a red light.

Because of the circumstances, the judge had sentenced her to minimum security and given her a minimum sentence. She'd served a little over four years.

***

Mandy showed me to a cell on the ground floor, it was where those serving short sentences, less than ten years, were housed. I was sharing with her and was pleased about that. There wasn't a lot of room, but then, I had nothing anyway. A cot stood against each wall and while one was made up, the other had linen, and what looked like a wardrobe of clothes folded neatly on it.

"That's your bed. You'll find you have four changes of clothes, underwear, toiletries and sleepwear. Personal hygiene products for one month are included and after that they have to be purchased. There's a list of everything you can buy. You fill in the form and drop it in the box by the guard's station. Orders are delivered every Tuesday afternoon. You'll be assigned a work detail in the next few days, until then, I suggest you offer to help where you can, get the other women onside."

"Do they......will they.....?"

"There are a few bullies who push and shove. Occasionally a woman gets beaten up, but in general they're not too bad. I guess maximum security would be where you'd be in danger of being badly beaten, raped. Most of those here aren't vicious but you still need to be careful."

Mandy spent the rest of the afternoon and early evening showing me around, teaching me the ropes until it was time for supper. I'd noted the curious looks being directed my way as we passed by, and when we entered the dining area, dozens of eyes scrutinized me, I felt heat rise in my face.

"Ignore them," Mandy said.

I followed Mandy to a table which had a few vacant seats and sat next to her. Within seconds, four other women moved closer. One sidled up next to me and fingered my hair. Chills ran down my spine and I shuffled closer to Mandy.

"Please, don't," I whispered.

"Lisa, leave her alone," Mandy ordered.

Lisa slid a little further away and I relaxed. Supper turned out to be a talkative affair as the women bombarded me with dozens of questions. I answered everything they asked, mostly with lies. As we left the hall to return to our cells, the girls followed, still asking questions. I felt threatened, but Mandy didn't seem concerned.

It turned out I had no reason to worry, the women peeled off as they neared their own cells after saying a pleasant goodnight.

I flopped down on my unmade bed and Mandy grinned at me. "Honey, you have about five minutes to get everything put away and the bed made before the guards come around for their nightly check. It won't be pleasant if they find it like that."

I jumped up from the bed and Mandy helped me get everything in order, thirty seconds later a guard by the name of Marcia poked her head in the door and introduced herself. TShe stopped short of welcoming me even though she made me feel welcome. I liked her and she was someone I thought I could go to if I was in trouble. I voiced my opinion to Mandy after Marcia had left.

"I like her, she seems nice."

"Most of the guards are, you can count on them for help if you need it."

"I thought they were supposed to be mean?"

"A couple are, but they're the exception. Lisa is mentally disabled so don't let her get to you, she doesn't mean any harm."

"Why is she here instead of an asylum?"

"She stabbed one of the other patients to death when the staff forgot to give her nighttime medications."

"Oh."

"The guards haven't missed for eight years, I doubt they'll start now." Mandy patted my hand. "Stop worrying."

A shout of *"lights out in ten"* echoed through the building and I heard the scrambling of women getting into bed. Mandy and I did the same. I had survived my first few hours in prison.

Chapter Seventeen

CALLIE

Two Months Later

Five fucking days in a row I'd puked my guts up. All day. Every day. I couldn't keep anything down. I hadn't felt well for a couple of months, but it hadn't been as bad as the past five days. Mandy was worried about me dehydrating. The doctor I visited said I had a *bug* and needed rest and fluids.

Newsflash...neither were working. I couldn't eat more than a handful of anything without puking and I wasn't sleeping. I was exhausted. When I collapsed outside my door, the guards organized approval from the warden for an ambulance to cart me to hospital. Marcia, the guard who'd been good to me since I'd arrived at the prison, stayed with me.

Doctors descended on me as soon as I was through the doors of the emergency room. I was poked, prodded, had blood taken, was scanned, and prodded some more. All the while, Marcia was nearby holding my hand. A drip was put in place after the doctor said I was severely dehydrated. Halfway through her going over the test results with me, my stomach churned, I felt like I was on fire and puked all over myself. I was sorry for the nurses who were tasked to clean up the foul-smelling bile. I'd never felt so ill in my life.

Once clean, with fresh sheets, and what the doctor called *safe* medications, she started explaining again.

I felt drowsy, her voice droned in my ears, but then one word had me snapping to attention, taking notice.

"....so, Ms. Green, your illness is due to you being pregnant."

"What?"

"You're two and a half months pregnant and are suffering with severe morning sickness. It's unusual for it to begin at this stage in the pregnancy, normally it ends around this time."

I was speechless. Sure, I hadn't had periods but that was nothing unusual, they'd always been erratic. And I was on the fucking pill! So many conflicting emotions assaulted my mind and body.

My hand moved to settle over my belly which showed no sign of swelling yet. I was pregnant.

I was carrying Jake's baby. His son, or daughter, and it would be a part of my love to keep forever. I was no longer going to be alone.

Fuck! I had decisions to make regarding our future before we left prison. I had a child coming who would depend on me. My days of being bad, of being a useless member of society would have to come to an end.

"Are you okay?" the kindly doctor asked.

"Yes. I'm shocked because I was on the pill, so never considered pregnancy."

"The pill is known to fail now and again."

Of course it would. I felt like I was holding a fucking bingo card and wondered what would be thrown at me next.

Drug addict mother killed. Check.

Foster family slave. Check.

Adoptive father killed. Check.

Evil uncle. Check.

Beatings. Check.

First man who loved me killed. Check.

Prison. Check.

Unexpected pregnancy. Check.

B.I.N.G.O. For fuck sake!

Marcia asked the next question. " How long do you need to keep her here? Can you treat the illness?"

"We'll keep her here until the medications take effect and she's stable. I want her hydrated before she leaves. The medications we use are new but proven safe for baby. They are shown to keep the nausea and vomiting under control although she may still experience periods of illness."

A baby. Jake's baby. Tears sprang to my eyes and Marcia gathered me in her arms. She held me while I cried.

I cried for the baby. I cried for Jake and the fact he'd never know his son or daughter. I cried for me and the responsibility I now shouldered.

Once again, my fucked up life was being turned upside down but I was determined to take care of my baby.

***

Four Months Later

I waddled in for breakfast, at six and a half months pregnant, I was huge. This baby would be born at the age of two going on its size. The chronic illness was being managed very well with the medication I'd been given and now I only had the odd bad day where I found myself kneeling and praying to the porcelain gods.

The past months, since returning from hospital had been a hell of a lot better than the first two. Once news got out about my pregnancy, thanks to Marcia, the bullying, pushing, shoving, and threats had pretty much stopped. Verbal abuse was still thrown my way, but never developed into anything physical. The women in the place weren't hardened criminals, they were like me, paying for one stupid mistake. One bad split-second decision. None of them would do anything to harm a baby. In fact, the opposite had happened, many of them started mothering me.

I sat in my allotted place at the table and Mandy dropped into a chair beside me.

"I'm gonna miss you kid, stay in touch?"

"I will." Tears sprang to my eyes. I felt like someone on death row, this was to be my last meal inside.

After breakfast I had a meeting with Warden Sharpe and then would be turned back onto the streets. Not a damn thing had changed, I still had nowhere to go.

Oh, one thing had changed, I had Jake's baby growing inside me. If I said I wasn't terrified, I'd be lying. I did have a few changes of clothes and a large layette for the baby thanks to the women I'd spent the past six months with. They'd spent their time in the sewing room making sure I'd have enough to hold me over. I was so grateful to them.

"Scared?" Mandy's voice broke into my thoughts.

"Terrified." I rested a hand over my belly and jerked when the baby kicked. It was definitely going to be a footballer and I hoped it would be a boy. I wanted him to look just like Jake. I'd been tempted to learn the sex at my last scan but I held firm in my resolve to be surprised.

Mandy lay a hand over mine when I pushed the bowl of cereal away. I was too worried to eat; my stomach was in knots. It was a dilemma because I knew I should eat for the baby's sake if not mine. Fuck knew where my next meal would come from.

"Marcia said Warden Sharpe is aware of your situation. Word is, she always makes sure the women here have somewhere to go and support until they're back on their feet."

"I hope she can help because right now I have next to no money, no family or friends on the outside, and a baby due in less than two and a half months.

I dragged the cereal back in front of me and ate. Every mouthful seemed to lodge in my throat before finally making its way into my stomach.

***

An hour later, I stood outside the warden's door, my small bag of belongings in one hand, purse in the other. The guard knocked and Warden Sharpe called out for us to enter. I'd only had occasion to speak to the woman twice before, she'd been firm, stern, but fair. She glanced up and smiled as I entered the room, it put me at ease. The guard closed the door and stayed outside.

"Take a seat, Callie."

I placed the bag on the floor and sat in a chair across the desk from the warden. She leaned forward, elbows on the desk, her fingers entwined. She studied me closely.

"Do you have somewhere to go?"

I shook my head, tears burned my eyes.

The warden reached over and patted my arm. "Let me tell you a story."

I nodded and accepted the tissue she offered, wiping the tears away.

"A couple of years ago, within a month of each other, two men were released from Fisher Maximum Security Prison. I won't go into too many details but one of those men, Tyler Warner had been wrongly convicted of embezzlement which had been committed by his brother. He suffered terribly inside, almost lost his life. His now husband, Bailey Warner, had been his Peer Inmate, and they fell in love. Tyler was acquitted when an auditor found proof it had been his brother who had committed the crime. When his brother and mother were killed in a plane crash, Tyler inherited the money authorities found in a South American bank along with the family business."

Warden Sharpe paused.

"He didn't want the business so it was sold. He purchased a motel, had it renovated and converted to a center for released prisoners with nowhere to go. It's called Beyond the Bars, The Tyler Warner Center for wrongly convicted prisoners. It's run by Jane and Peter Warner. Bailey is a Clinical Psychologist with his own practice, and his husband, Tyler manages the business side of it. Bailey offers his services free of charge to the center and his mother, Jane, calls him in when she feels he's needed."

"I was guilty though so how does this help me?"

"About six months after the center opened, the family realized the court system was doing its job very well and most of the time the facility was empty. Tyler and Bailey weren't prepared to give it up so when they found out how many prisoners had no-one and nowhere to go on release, they turned it into a facility for them. They will help you to find housing and advise you of services you can apply for."

Warden Sharpe handed me a card.

"Go and see them. Jane will make sure you and your baby don't end up on the streets."

Tears dripped down my cheeks at the woman's kindness. I couldn't believe I had someone to turn to, someone who could help. I mean she wouldn't send me there otherwise, would she?

She stood, and using the desk, I pushed onto my feet. "Thank you, Warden Sharpe."

The warden gave me a hug, handed me my bag and purse, and led me to the door. When it opened, the guard stood waiting on the other side.

"Stay out of trouble, Callie, you don't belong here."

I nodded as the guard led me away. Freedom.

***

I stood staring at the glass door leading into the center, hands rested over my swollen belly.

"Well, kiddo. It's just you and me in this fucked up world. Let's hope the warden was right and this place can help us. If not, we're out on the streets."

I sucked in a deep breath, waddled up to the door and pushed inside. A pretty lady, seated behind a counter, smiled at me and stood. She passed through a door at the end of the counter and approached me.

"Can I help you, sweetheart? My name is Jane."

Her soft, caring voice washed over me and tears filled my eyes. "My name is Callie. The warden said you could help. Please help me, I have nowhere to go and no-one to turn to."

"Oh, honey." Jane stepped forward and drew me into her arms.

The dam burst and I sobbed my heart out. I clung onto the hope that this lady was my much-needed lifeline. If not, my child and I were doomed.

Chapter Eighteen

CALLIE

Jane coaxed me to a sofa positioned by the wall and I sat down. While I scrubbed the tears from my face, she poured me a cup of water from a fountain nearby. After handing it to me, she picked up my bag and placed it beside me.

"I need to go and ask my husband to come out and look after things. I'll take you to one of the units where we can talk privately and where you'll be staying.

I nodded and Jane disappeared through a door off to one side of the reception counter. When she returned, she had a tall handsome man following her, and a notebook and pen in one hand. The man smiled down at me, he had a warm, friendly face.

"This is my husband, Peter. We'll both be around if you need us, we live in a cottage at the back of the units."

"Hi Callie. You're safe here, we'll take care of you and your baby." Peter assured.

"Thank you," I whispered.

"Okay, let's get you settled." Jane gathered my hand and helped me onto my feet. I needed it these days.

She scooped up my bag, wrapped her hand around my elbow and led me outside. Behind the reception area was a row of blue doors.

"There are ten units here."

Jane guided me to a door with a brass number '2' in the center and swiped a card in a slot. A green light flashed and she pushed the door open. We both stepped inside and the door silently closed behind us.

The unit was small but bright and clean. There was a large bed flanked with side tables and on the brick wall above were fixed reading lights. On the wall opposite was a unit with a flat screen television on the wall above. To the left was a desk and swivel chair, next to that, a small kitchenette. I noted a door opposite.

"Bathroom," Jane said when she saw where I was looking.

"This is lovely."

"My son and son-in-law are responsible for the place, we manage it for them. Sit down, honey."

I plonked myself down on the bed beside my bag. Jane pulled up the chair from the desk and sat in front of me. She opened the notebook and removed a sheet of paper which she handed to me.

"This is a list of rules and emergency contact numbers. The main rules while you're here are: no alcohol or drugs and no-one stays over."

"I understand, you won't have a problem with any of these things where I'm concerned."

"Normally we give you a week to settle in and then my daughter Mykayla would escort you to the unemployment office to start looking for work."

"You trust ex-prisoners alone with your daughter?"

Jane laughed. "Absolutely not. She has Calvin with her at all times. He's trained in the Martial Arts, tall, and built like a brick wall. Oh, and he carries a gun. Anyway, she'll take you to the benefits office to sort out housing and other entitlements. Work will need to come later for you."

"Thank you."

"We have a dining area and kitchen where you can make your own meals. We keep it fully stocked. We encourage you to come up and mingle with the other residents. We have eight at the moment—five men and three women including you. We also have a recreation room and I encourage you to spend time there even if it's only for a chat. It helps with loneliness."

"I might after I've had a few days to settle."

"You won't be pushed but I really don't want you locking yourself away in your unit."

"How long do I have before I have to get out?"

"As long as you need, up to a year."

A whole year of stability, I'd never had that.

"Now, I've learned from the past to be nosy, get to really know the people here. Sadly, when we first started the center, we didn't want to interfere other than pointing people in the direction of finding work and filling in forms. We pretty much left our residents alone. Then, we had a suicide so now I'm a busybody who is up in everyone's business. I check on you twice a day so I can be alerted to any problems before they spiral out of control."

"Seems reasonable, but I have so many problems, I'm already out of control."

"Tell me, why were you in prison and for how long?"

"I stole a car, didn't have a license because I had no idea how to drive, and endangered lives. I was in for six months."

Jane burst into laughter and she must have noted the confusion I felt on my face. "You'd never driven but you stole a car?"

She laughed again and I laughed with her. It was pretty funny.

"I know it sounds pretty stupid now, but my boyfriend had just died and I wasn't thinking straight. I wanted to get out of Foster and go to a bigger city."

"Haven't you heard of buses?"

"Yeah, I couldn't take the bus."

To her credit, Jane didn't pry.

"I'm sorry you lost your boyfriend, was he the baby's father?"

"Yes."

She patted my knee as tears flowed over my cheeks.

"I still miss him so much, I'm just not getting over it."

"I know, honey. I'll leave you to get some rest and I'll bring you lunch a little later. We'll go up to the dining room for supper. I'm going to insist you have a chat with my son, Bailey. He's in the medical field, I'll ask him to come down tomorrow."

"He's a Psychologist?"

"Yes, how did you know."

"Warden Sharpe told me when she explained about the center. I'll talk with him if you think it will help."

"I do, honey. I think you're at risk of falling into a deep depression if you don't talk about what's happened."

"I'll talk with him if it stays between us."

"I promise you, it will."

Maybe it would do me good to talk about my past, about Jake and what I'd seen. Even after six months, it was eating me alive. The murder trial would be over so I wouldn't be called as a witness and I was pretty sure the club members wouldn't want me now. I heard somewhere that doctors are like priests, that what I say will remain between the two of us. Hopefully he'll be able to help me move on because at that moment I was treading water and in danger of drowning.

"Get some rest, honey, I'll be back in an hour or so."

***

A soft knock woke me, and I awkwardly hefted my whale sized body from the bed, padded across the carpeted floor, and swung the door open. Jane stood before me, a smile on her beautiful face, a tray in her hands.

"Lunch. Chicken salad and chocolate mousse. I brought you 4 bottles of water and a carton of milk for coffee or tea. I'll put them in your fridge."

Talking of food set my stomach churning and I realized I'd forgotten to take my medication at breakfast. I pushed past Jane, she squeaked in shock at my rudeness but I was in a hurry to get to the bathroom.

I rushed through the door, dropped to my knees, lifted the lid and emptied what was left in my stomach from breakfast into the pan. Jane held my hair back while I dry-wretched. Once I felt a little better, I sat back on my heels. Jane reached for a cloth, wet it under the faucet and gently cleaned my face. After flushing the toilet, she helped me onto my feet. I was unsteady and nauseous. Jane held me until we reached the bed and I lay down.

She sat on the bed beside me and mopped the sweat from my face with the damp, cool cloth.

"You're sick, honey. I'll call for a doctor. We can't take the chance of it being something serious while you're pregnant."

Jane started to stand but I reached out and grasped her arm.

"No doctor." I felt as weak as a newborn and wanted to sleep. "Pills in my purse."

Jane glared at me, a deep frown on her face. I realized immediately, she thought I was an addict.

"Severe form of morning sickness. Doctor at the hospital said I'll have it all day every day until the baby is born. The pills help control it for the most part, but I forgot to take one this morning and last night's has probably worn off."

I watched as her frown disappeared and the glare was replaced with a look of concern. She visibly relaxed before standing and going for my purse which I'd left on the desk. She came back with the box of pills and a bottle of water. I popped the medication and had a long drink. The cooling water soothed the burn in my throat caused by the acid from puking. Jane wiped my face again with the cloth.

"How long do you have left, honey?"

"About eight weeks I think."

"You're very big."

"Tell me about it. I have another scan due and I'm convinced they'll tell me I'm carrying a two-year-old."

Jane burst into laughter but I was partially serious.

"The doctor at the prison contacted Dr. Metcalfe to look after me and I see him at the end of next week." I had no fucking idea how I was going to pay for it and my hospital stay was going to be very, very short.

"Would you like me to come with you? We could get a bite to eat and visit the office to organize your benefits."

"I'd like that, thank you."

"You're welcome, honey. You don't have a mother?"

I shook my head. "She was shot dead in a bar when she was caught in an argument between gang members."

"I'm so sorry, honey."

"Don't be, she wasn't much of a mother. Are you always so kind to the people who come here?"

"I like to think so." Jane patted my leg and stood. "I'll put the lunch in your fridge so it's there if you get hungry later. Rest, and I'll be back for you at supper."

"Thank you." My eyelids were heavy and I felt myself drifting off.

The door closed with a soft click.

***

I woke the following morning feeling much better and my thoughts drifted to the previous evening.

I'd enjoyed a light supper with Peter, Jane, and their daughter Mykayla. To say she was gorgeous wouldn't do her justice, I'd never seen such a beautiful girl. I learned she was only a few months older than me, but oh, how different.

I'd met six of the other residents, four men and two women. They were all much older than me, but seemed friendly and welcoming. After we'd eaten, I was shown through to the recreation room where there was a pool table, a small table with two chairs and a chess set, a ping pong table and several other small tables which could be used for playing one of the boxed games. They had a huge selection which were packed neatly into a cupboard. There were also cards, dominoes, and a cribbage board. Most of it I'd never seen before and had no idea how they were played. They had certainly provided plenty of entertainment for those who wanted it.

I was also shown the laundry area which had four large machines and four dryers. Cleaning powders and liquids were all provided. I felt like I'd fallen from Hell and landed in Heaven.

Mykayla had walked me back to the unit and stayed for a while. She chatted about her big brother, Bailey, his husband, Tyler and their six-month-old baby, Justin Peter. To hear her gush about them, it was obvious she was besotted with them all, especially her nephew. I'd found myself wishing I had a loving family like theirs.

I sighed and waddled to the bathroom for a hot shower. I'd almost had the family I craved with Jake and Maree before it had been so cruelly snatched away. I felt guilty about not being in touch with Maree, but she wouldn't want me around now, a reminder of the brother she'd lost. It nagged at me constantly that she'd never get to know Jake's child, her nephew or niece. Maybe in a year or two when the grief wasn't so raw.

Once showered and dried, I dressed and headed to the dining hall for breakfast. I was pleased when I managed both cereal and toast, I was surprisingly hungry. I was joined by a woman called Mona who I'd met the previous night, and a man called Jeff I hadn't met before. The conversation was easy and interesting.

As I sipped at my mug of tea, Jane entered the room holding a beautiful baby. He had a thick thatch of black hair. She was flanked by two amazingly handsome men. They were both tall and muscular. One had sandy brown hair, the other man's hair was as black as coal like the child. These men were obviously Bailey and Tyler but I had no idea who was who.

When they approached me, I excused myself, pushed up from the chair and waddled toward them. Once close, I knew which man was Bailey. He had the same piercing green eyes and sandy brown hair as his mother and sister, Tyler's eyes were pale gray. The baby gazed at me, his eyes were also a bright green.

Introductions were made and small talk about Justin followed until he began to fuss.

"He's tired, mom. Kept us up half the night, with his teething. I'll put him down for a nap while you and Bailey take care of Callie." Tyler turned to me. "We have a crib in mom's office for when we're here."

I nodded my understanding.

Jane handed her grandson over. He burrowed his little head into his daddy's shoulder and sucked on his thumb. His eyes were already closed. Tyler held him close while Bailey rubbed the child's back, the scene brought tears to my eyes, it was beautiful. The men kissed and I watched as Tyler walked away.

"There's a small room off the recreation room, we can talk there privately with no interruptions." Bailey led the way, and while he closed the door, Jane and I sat on a sofa. Bailey reached for a notebook and pen from the small desk before sitting in the chair opposite.

Jane gathered my hand in hers, I felt safe.

"Okay, Callie. You don't need to tell me anything which makes you uncomfortable. I'd like to know your background, it would help me make a more accurate decision on what I can do to help, but I won't force you to tell me anything. Whatever you say, doesn't leave this room.

"I think if you know my story, you'll understand why I feel so helpless, powerless to do anything."

I proceeded to tell Bailey everything. Yep, every sordid detail. Talk about verbal diarrhea.

When I got to the part about escaping from Ray and meeting Jake, I paused. Jane was squeezing my hand, and when I glanced at her, I found her eyes full of tears, some dripped onto her cheeks. Bailey's eyes reflected sadness. After taking a deep breath, I talked about how Jake had found me and taken me to his sister's place.

"Jake, President of the Free Lords MC?" Bailey asked.

"Yes. He was wonderful and I fell completely in love with him. I'd never been happier, there was a light at the end of the tunnel."

"The baby is his?"

"Yes, I've never been with another man and never will be." I patted my belly. "At least I'll have a piece of Jake to love."

"So, what happened, why did you leave?"

"About six months ago I arrived at the club to find Jake on the floor, blood pouring from a gunshot wound in his shoulder. One of the members with him said he was dead. I ran."

Bailey gave me a strange look. I explained about belonging to the other members once Jake was dead, and how I couldn't allow that to happen, so I'd had to leave town. I also explained how I was terrified of being called as a witness against the man who'd shot him, I'd seen the gun in his hand.

"So, I needed to get to a bigger city away from Foster. I stole a car, even though I didn't know how to drive, got caught, and ended up in prison. Now you know it all. Every detail of my fucked up, miserable life. Maybe I am bad and that's why bad things happen to me." I brushed at the tears on my cheeks.

Bailey's voice was soft and hoarse. My story had obviously touched this lovely man. "I've heard some horror stories in my time, hell, I watched my husband suffer untold pain, but as bad as it was, it only lasted for a short time. Yours has lasted a lifetime, I understand why you feel the way you do, why you want to give up. What do you plan to do?"

"I have no idea. I have no-one which is why I'm here. I'm scared to death of what might happen to me, and my baby, but I'd kill us both before I become my mother."

Jane squeezed my hand hard.

"We won't let that happen. I know everything you've said is between you, me, and mom. I promised you that confidentiality, but I know someone who can help you a hell of lot more than I can if you'll give me permission to tell your story."

"Why not, I'm past caring anymore. If you think it will help, go ahead."

I turned to Jane who was staring at her son with a strange expression on her face.

"Callie, will you head back to your unit while I speak with mom? I'll be down to see you in a couple of hours." Bailey helped me onto my feet and I closed the door before waddling away.

Chapter Nineteen

BAILEY

We sat quietly until Callie left the room and closed the door. Mom spoke first.

"Jake Prescott? He's the man you know can help Callie?"

I was at school with Jake, and even though he's a couple of years younger than me we know each other to talk to and his club does a lot for the underprivileged of Foster.

"I have to tell him, mom. You know he's had men out looking for her for months, and word is he's now hired a private investigator. Word is he's not the same since she went missing, and it's breaking Callie's heart thinking he's dead. I'm worried about her mental health."

"She's been through far too much in her life, she deserves a chance at happiness."

"Jake will give her the love and family she craves and she deserves to know he's alive. He obviously loves her deeply or he wouldn't have kept searching."

"Go and tell him, son. Put their lives back together."

I pushed up from the chair and mom stood. She wrapped her arms around me in a hug and kissed my cheek.

We headed back to reception to let Tyler know I had something I needed to take care of. We found him with coffee in hand, talking with dad. My man's face lit up in a smile when he saw me, but then he frowned, put the coffee mug down and took two long strides toward me. He gathered me in his arms and I lowered my head against the muscle of his chest. He kissed the top of my head and I felt a few tears escape. When he placed fingers under my chin and tilted my head back, I saw the concern in his gorgeous gray eyes.

"What's wrong, babe?"

I swallowed hard. "I just heard the most gut-wrenching life story. It broke my heart, Tyler. No-one should ever be treated the way Callie has been. I thought what you suffered was bad enough, but Callie has suffered at the hands of monsters for every minute of her eighteen years."

Tyler brushed his lips over mine and thumbed away my tears. "I'm so sorry, babe. Is there anything we can do to help?"

"I know someone who can help her better than I can, I need to go out for a while."

"Do you want me to come with you? I'm sure mom would be happy to take care of Justin."

I glanced around and noted mom and dad have left us to talk alone.

"No, baby. This is doctor/patient confidential. As much as I would love you to come with me, I can't betray Callie's confidence."

"I understand. I'll stay here so mom can fuss over Justin and I'll catch up on some computer work. He might be little but our son sure commands a lot of attention."

I chuckled. Tyler was guilty of spoiling Justin, but then so was I. He'd been such a well behaved, gentle baby. I hoped Melissa would be our surrogate again when we were ready for our next child, she assured us she would be."

"Thanks, baby." I love my man more every day, he's my whole life, my world. I couldn't imagine life without him.

"Always here for you, babe."

We embraced and kissed deeply before I walked away.

***

The clubhouse was quiet when I entered, it was mid-morning so I assumed most of the members were working.

A man approached me with a scowl on his face. Wow, I'm a tall man and muscular but this guy was huge. Believe me when I say, you did not want to get on his wrong side. He looked me up and down, and when he spoke, his voice was gruff, his expression suspicious.

"What do you want?"

Hmm, no pleasant greeting, not that I expected it. I'd invaded their turf. "Is Jake in?"

"Why?"

This guy was like a fucking Rottweiler guarding its pups. When you're part of a motorcycle club, and a stranger invades your space, I guess you have to be.

"I have something important to discuss with him."

"Such as?"

Fuck, this man doesn't make it easy. I threw him a bone.

"It's about Callie. I'm Bailey, her Psychologist."

That got his attention, he suddenly had hold of my arm and I was being dragged through the clubhouse. "I'm Viking Dave, you're lucky Pres is in his office checking emails. Normally he's left for the shop by now."

I was taken to a door at the end of the hallway. He knocked once, flung the door open and pulled me inside. Jake glanced up from his computer screen, confusion etched on his face.

"Warner, what are you doing here?"

"He has news about Callie, Pres."

Jake leapt from his chair and rounded the desk. "Where the fuck is she?"

I shrugged Viking's hand from my arm and stepped back. "I need to speak with you privately, Prescott."

"Viking is my VP, he can hear what you have to say."

I glared at Jake. "No. He. Can't. Callie confided in me as her Psychologist. I have permission from her to speak with someone I said could help. She doesn't know that someone is you, Prescott. I won't break her confidence. If Viking doesn't leave, I will."

Jake lifted his chin and the VP left the room. I closed the door behind him.

"Sit." Jake indicated a sofa and we both sat. "Talk, where the fuck is she? I've had men searching for her for months. Shit, we've turned every town within a hundred-mile radius upside down and there's been nothing. It was like she'd vanished into thin air. Even a PI I hired a week ago hasn't been able to find her. How the fuck did you?"

"She found us. Callie was in prison, Jake, she got out yesterday and came to our center for help. Mom was concerned about her state of mind and called me in to speak with her. I saw her this morning."

"Prison? Why the fuck was she in prison?"

I explained to Jake about Callie and what happened after she thought he was dead. "She couldn't face being a club woman so she stole a car to get away."

"Club woman? She would never be a fucking club woman. Why the fuck would she think that? And, she can't drive, why the hell did she steal a car?"

"Callie was desperate. She told me she'd just lost the love of her life and would never allow another man to touch her that way. She was also terrified of being called as a witness to your murder and thought your men would get hold of her if she was."

"Fuck. I want to see her. I need to explain." The big, tough President biker had tears in his eyes.

"That's why I'm here. I'm worried about her. Callie is deeply depressed and I'm afraid she'll quit fighting and give up."

"I won't let her give up. I love that woman with every cell in my body. I've been going out of my mind not knowing where she is. I've spent every waking hour looking for her. I've even put notices all over the internet. I want her back in my arms, my bed, my home. Fuck, I wanna make her my wife."

"I'm relieved to hear you feel that way because she needs you now more than ever." I stare into Jake's glassy eyes. "She's pregnant with your baby, Jake and due to give birth in around eight weeks."

Jake sprang to his feet. "Take me to her. NOW!"

***

JAKE

Viking Dave was at the end of the hall when I left the office. "I'll be out for the rest of the day and tomorrow. Fuck. I'll be back whenever. Unless it's a matter of life or death, no-one calls me. Take care of everything."

"You okay?" Viking Dave was concerned, he knew how much I'd suffered since Callie had gone missing. My bad girl had broken my damn heart.

"It's about to be."

I hurried from the club, Bailey hot on my heels.

"Are you sure you don't want to come with me, Prescott?"

"Nope, I'll get the truck. I'll need it to take her home."

Bailey nodded and headed for his town car while I strode to my truck—a black Chevy Pickup. I slid into the driver's seat and the engine roared to life with the turn of a key. I eased onto the road behind Bailey.

Twenty minutes later, I screeched to a stop in the parking area of *Beyond The Bars*. I couldn't believe my woman had been in prison, she must have been fucking terrified.

Bailey joined me when I stepped from the truck. "Stay calm, Prescott. Callie is going to get the shock of her life when she sees you're alive."

"I'll try," I answered.

Bailey led me to a door embellished with a brass number '2'. He pushed me off to the side and knocked softly. I heard movement inside and the door was thrust open. It was true, my woman was here. She stood looking at Bailey with a smile on her face but her eyes were so sad.

My heart thumped in my chest. Callie. My Callie was here. My bad girl had finally been found. She was pale and her belly was huge with my baby.

My baby.

Our child.

I was gonna be a fucking father.

"I have someone here I think you'd like to see." Bailey stepped away from the door.

It was my cue to take his place. Callie's eyes widened, the shock of seeing me obvious. Her hands flew to her mouth.

"Jake."

It was barely a whisper, and the only word she muttered before collapsing into my arms. I scooped her up, laid her on the bed in the small unit, and sat on the bed beside her.

Bailey hurried from the room and returned with a damp cloth which he placed over her forehead. I grasped her hands in mine as if my very life depended on the connection with her.

"She'll be fine. Let her wake up in her own time. I'll be at reception if you need me."

Bailey turned to leave but when I called his name, he glanced over his shoulder.

"Thank you for giving Callie back to me."

He nodded. "She needs you, Jake."

A moment later he was gone and the door whooshed closed. I stood, removed my jacket and boots, and climbed onto the bed where I pulled Callie into my arms.

She rolled onto her side, lay her head on my chest and flung an arm across my waist. Her belly rested against my side and I felt a sharp kick to my ribs. Tears filled my eyes. My baby was kicking his daddy.

Chapter Twenty

CALLIE

Something big and warm has me locked in a vice like grip, my head was settled against a wall of muscle. I almost snuggled closer but then it hit me. Jake! Was I dreaming he was here? Alive!

I slowly opened my eyes, lifted my head and gazed straight into Jake's chocolate brown eyes. I gasped, my stomach somersaulted and my heart skipped a beat. I was frozen in place, too scared to move in case he disappeared, and I found out it was only a dream.

"You're dead," I whispered.

Jake chuckled. "I hope not. Ratchet proved to be a lousy shot when he's nervous, and I lost a lot of blood, but I'm very much alive."

We rolled onto our sides and faced each other. Jake reached a hand behind my head and drew me forward for a kiss. I melted against him for a moment before drawing away.

"Why did Ratchet shoot you? I heard Slider say you were dead."

Jake held my hand and explained the set-up to catch the men who had been betraying the

Panthers. "When I heard you scream, I wanted to hold you and tell you I was okay but I passed out.

When I woke in the hospital, Viking Dave said he had men out looking for you. I knew they'd find you so I wasn't worried. Psycho was, and still is, a fucking mess. He blamed himself for you going to the club and seeing what happened. He had no idea you'd go there. He thought you would leave work and head home. We didn't want you caught up in our set-up which is why I had you working downtown." He sighed deeply. "I probably should have told you what we had planned, but I didn't want you worried. It seemed you'd fucking vanished off the face of the earth, so a few days ago I hired a PI. He hadn't been able to find a damn thing either."

"I'm sorry, Jake. I remembered you telling me if something happened to Slider that Sally would become a club woman. I couldn't bear the thought of becoming a club woman and having other men touching me. So, I ran and stayed out of sight when I saw the men searching."

Jake ran his hand down my arm. "Sweetheart, that was never going to happen."

"But, you said....."

"You were never going to be a club woman, Sally would because she would want to be. The men would have taken care of you, made sure you had a home and anything else you needed. Once the president's woman, always the president's woman. They don't force women to be with them, I'd have them out of the club in the blink of an eye if they did. We might be rough around the edges and do things we shouldn't, but we're not monsters."

Tears flooded my eyes, I'd been so stupid. "I didn't know, and I didn't want anyone else touching me the way you did...ever."

Jake wiped away my tears and lowered his mouth over mine, as the kiss deepened the baby gave a hard kick to Jake's ribs. He drew back sharply.

"Wow buddy, nice kick to daddy's ribs."

I laughed, feeling insanely happy for the first time in months. I had Jake back in my arms, and if this was a dream, I didn't ever want to wake up. "It's gonna play football."

"Do you know what it is?"

"No, I wanted it to be a surprise. I have a scan due, we can find out if you want to know."

"Nah, a surprise will be nice. I can't believe I'm gonna be a father. I can't wait to call ma and dad. Maree will be over the moon. Marry me."

Um, did I hear right? What did he just ask? "What?"

"Marry me. I love you, Callie and I never want to lose you again."

Tears streamed down my face. "I love you so much. My whole world fell apart when I thought you were dead. If it wasn't for our baby, I don't know if I'd still be here. If you're sure, yes, I'll marry you."

Jake let out a shout which startled me and caused the baby to kick hard. He pulled me closer into his arms and kissed the breath from my lungs. I could barely breathe by the time he released me, but what bliss.

"I'll get a license tomorrow. Do you want a big wedding?"

"No, I only want you. I've never wanted all the frills and fuss."

"We'll have it in Maree's backyard, she'll be thrilled. I'll call her."

"Jake, slow down, honey. We have plenty of time, I'm not going anywhere. I won't steal anymore cars."

"Yeah, we'll get to that. No, you're not going anywhere without me ever again, but I want us married before the baby arrives."

"If you're sure, you don't want more time to think about it?"

"Nope. I've never been more sure of anything in my life. It broke my heart not being able to find you. Come on, I'll help you pack and take you home where you belong."

Home. It sounded so good.

Jake helped me from the bed. I crossed to the small closet and pulled out my bag. When I reached back in for clothing, Jake took the bag from my hands, sat me down on the bed and commenced packing for me. Once done he zipped the bag and glanced around.

"Is that it?"

"Except for my toothbrush and hairbrush in the bathroom. I left in a hurry and didn't take anything with me. Those things including the bag are what the women in prison made for me and the baby when they knew I had nothing."

Jake entered the bathroom, brought back the brushes and tucked them into an outside pocket on the bag. He looked thoughtful. "I can't believe you stole a car. You must have been terrified of the men to have taken such a chance."

"Desperate. I didn't know them well enough to trust, Jake."

"I'm so sorry, sweetheart."

"It's not your fault."

He grasped my hand, helped me up from the bed, picked up the bag and we left the unit.

***

Jake wrapped his arm around me as we headed to reception to thank Jane and the others. Peter glanced up from the desk when we pushed through the glass door and entered.

"Jane. Bailey. Tyler," he shouted out.

The three of them came through the door a moment later, Justin was in Jane's arms.

"You're going home?" Bailey asked.

I glanced up at Jake and he smiled down at me.

"Yes, I'm going home. I can never thank you enough for what you have done for me and my baby, especially you, Bailey."

"You're welcome, honey," Jane said before handing Justin to Tyler and crushing me in a hug. "Stay in touch and bring baby to see us."

"I promise I will." I brushed tears from my eyes.

Bailey stepped up next and hugged me. "Good luck, honey. I'm glad you have your man back."

"Thanks to you."

Tyler handed Justin over to Jane and gave me a hug.

"Good luck."

I thanked him and Peter gave me a hug and said they would always be there if I needed them. They were a wonderful family, and despite the circumstances, I was honored to know them.

Jake shook hands with them all and thanked them for taking care of me. When it came Bailey's turn, he was pulled into a crushing hug.

"I'll never be able to thank you enough, Warner."

"Seeing you two together is thanks enough. I'm glad I remembered who you were when Callie mentioned your name."

With tears in mine, and Jane's eyes, Jake led me to his truck, lifted me in and we started for home.

***

Life back with Jake was like being caught in a whirlwind, when the others found out I was home, they all visited. Each one of them chastised me for running away but understood my fear. I realized now, it was totally unfounded.

Psycho lectured me, squeezed the life out of me, and lectured me some more. Even the Prospects turned up and assured me, no matter what happened in the future, I'd be safe and looked after. Everyone patted my belly and proclaimed themselves uncles. Our child was lucky to have these men to protect him. These big, bad bikers who unjustly put the fear of God into people when they were out on the street, had hearts of gold.

Tonight, they were all at our house including Maree, Mitch, and the girls.

I sat on the back veranda with my swollen feet raised on a stool and reflected on how lucky it was that I'd confided in Bailey. He'd given me my man back.

Jake and I were scheduled for a scan at the hospital the following day. Dr. Metcalfe was concerned with my size and the swelling in my ankles. The medication wasn't working as well either. My poor man hadn't known what to do when three days ago I spent half the night in the bathroom puking my guts up. He'd held my hair back, paced the floor in between my throwing up, and watched me like a hawk when I felt well enough to take a bath. I could see he was worried and it took all my soothing to prevent him from calling an ambulance. My big bear was actually more of a pussy cat.

I glanced over to where he stood grilling steaks while chatting with VP and Slider. A moment later he must have sensed me watching because his eyes met mine and his face lit up with a smile. Gosh, I loved my man and we seemed to have some kind of ethereal connection.

"How are you doing, honey?" Maree pulled up a chair, sat beside me and gathered my hand in hers.

I thought I'd been lectured and admonished by Jake and his men but it was nothing compared to the dressing down Maree had given me. We'd no sooner arrived home than she was on the doorstep. She'd taken me into her arms and hugged me fiercely while we both shed gallons of tears. Nope, Maree was not a woman I'd like to be on the wrong side of for real.

"I've been better, I'll be glad when this baby is out."

Maree laughed. "I know what you mean, it seems the last month is the hardest. Jake tells me you've been really sick, he's worried about you."

"I've been sick on and off since I hit the two and a half month mark. Medication helped up until the past few days. Now, the mere smell of food makes me puke."

Maree patted my hand. "It'll be over soon and will all be worth it when you hold your baby in your arms."

"I know, I keep telling myself that."

"Jake finally let me see the nursery now it's finished; it's gorgeous."

"He's done most of it and I swear he would have bought everything in the store if I hadn't been there to stop him."

"My brother will be a good father."

"Yes, he will be, I've seen how good he is with the girls. I just hope I can be a good mother."

"You'll be fine. Mom and dad are flying in the week before you're due and mom's terrific. She has a way of being helpful without interfering. I don't know how I would have coped without her."

"I'm nervous about meeting them, what if they don't like me? Jake tells me not to worry, he said they'll love me."

A gust of wind blew the aroma of grilling steaks my way and my stomach dry heaved. Maree took hold of my arm, pulled me onto my feet and hurried me through to the bathroom. We barely had time to lift the lid on the toilet when I started to empty the contents of my stomach. When I had a slight break in the heaving, I lowered myself onto my knees. When I hit the floor, I realized I'd wet myself and struggled back to my feet. It was then I was hit by the most excruciating pain I'd felt in my life.

I grabbed my rolling belly, latched onto Maree to stop from falling and screamed out in agony. A second pain followed hot on the heels of the first and I screamed out again. When I glanced down at the floor, blood pooled at my feet. I was terrified.

Jake charged into the room.

Maree took over. "Get her on the bed, the baby's coming. I'll call for an ambulance but she won't make the hospital."

I screamed when another pain crippled me and had me doubling over—I was obviously a screamer when it came to giving birth, but right at that moment, I didn't give a fuck. My belly rose into the shape of a pyramid, pressure assaulted my pussy, and I didn't fight the urge to push. Even though in birthing classes I'd been told not to push until the doctor said it was safe.

Jake scooped me into his arms and hurried through to our guest room on the ground floor. He flung back the covers and placed me gently onto the mattress.

Maree rushed back into the room, lifted my dress and ripped off my panties. At that same time, another pain gripped me. I grabbed Jake's hand, my nails digging into his flesh.

"Make it go away, Jake."

He leaned over and kissed my forehead. "I wish I could, baby. It'll be over soon."

Not fucking soon enough. The urge to push was strong, I grunted, held my belly and felt my face heat as I held my breath and pushed with every ounce of strength I could find. The pain was one continuous ball now and I was almost demented with agony.

Jake lifted me up, sat on the side of the bed behind me and held me to his chest. I loved him with all my heart and knew he was hurting for me.

Maree was at the end of the bed, she had my knees bent and legs parted and was watching whatever was going on down there. "Fuck, I hope the paramedics get here soon, this baby is coming."

"Fuck, no, it can't come without a doctor, or someone who knows what they're doing."

I heard the panic in Jake's voice, and I didn't want to disappoint him, but his child was in one hell of a hurry to say hello to the world.

Maree kept telling me not to push like I had a choice. This baby didn't give a fuck whether I had a doctor or was in a hospital, he was coming when *he* was ready.

A siren wailed close by and then quieted. Seconds later two paramedics burst into the room just as the pain intensified, and the urge to push became overwhelming. I grunted, pushed, and grunted some more.

A female paramedic yelled at me to push hard. Finally, someone who was on the same page as me. I pushed back against Jake's chest and gave it everything I had, the baby slid from me and was laid on my stomach.

"Congratulations, you have a son. He's small, when were you due?" the female asked.

"Four weeks." I collapsed back against Jake, I was exhausted.

When I noticed the glance which passed between her and her partner, my heart leapt into my throat. "Is he okay?"

The female paramedic was checking him over, listening to his heart and clearing his throat. "He seems fine, just a bit on the small side. The staff at the hospital will check him out thoroughly and weigh him. I'm Kerry by the way and my partner is Gonzo."

"Gonzo?" I giggled.

"I have Italian parents," he growled by way of an explanation.

"Would dad like to cut the cord?" Kerry asked.

Jake set me back against the pillows, took the scissors from Kerry and cut where he was shown. Kerry lifted our son onto a towel that Maree was holding, and he damn near screamed the house down. He may have been small, but he sure had a good set of lungs. Jake and I would have no trouble hearing him when he woke in the night.

Maree wrapped him and handed him to me. Jake was seated on the side of the bed and he brushed his fingertips over the light brown hair which covered his head. To me, he looked just like his daddy. I birthed the placenta without incident and Gonzo placed it in a bag and labeled it to be weighed at the hospital.

I relaxed back against the pillows while our son dozed in my arms. Jake kissed me deeply, his love for me clear in his eyes.

"Do you have a name?" Kerry asked.

I shook my head, we hadn't had time to decide on one yet although we had a couple in mind.

"I'll just do a final check to make sure everything is okay and we'll transport you to the hospital." Kerry placed a gloved finger inside me and pressed on my belly, I noted her frown. "Did you know..."

She didn't finish what she was saying, a searing pain hit me, and I shrieked. At that moment, all hell broke loose. Our son bellowed,

Jake was yelling, and I added to the commotion when another pain hit me by screaming. I handed our son over to my man in case I dropped him onto the floor.

"What the fuck is happening to my woman?" Jake demanded to know.

"Jake, calm down, you're scaring the baby." Maree took him from her brother's arms, and handed him to Sally who was standing over in the corner looking scared to death. I hadn't known she was in the room but didn't mind. We were becoming good friends.

Kerry spoke sternly. "If everyone could just settle, I'll explain..."

Yep, poor Kerry couldn't finish a sentence. Another pain, another unearthly yell, and a strong urge to push. *Twins!* Why the fuck hadn't I been told?

"Why the fuck didn't the doctor tell me I was having twins?" I shouted before grunting and pushing.

"Sometimes one baby lies behind the other, and if they're not looking for a second baby, they don't see it. It's especially difficult if one baby is hidden behind the size of a normal singleton."

I yelled out again and pushed hard, it felt like I was being torn apart with this baby. Jake wrapped his arms around me and soothed me as the pushing got real.

"Fuck, Callie. Twins." He kissed my sweaty forehead. "I love you so much."

"I love you too," I grunted in between bearing down.

"Push harder, Callie," Kerry ordered.

Why the hell was she so calm when my insides were being shredded?

"Callie, push."

I leaned forward, glared at Kerry and pushed as hard as I could. Our second baby slid free and began screaming immediately, this set its brother off.

"Another boy, congratulations. Dad?"

Kerry held up the scissors and Jake again cut the cord. Our son was then placed in the towel Maree had at the ready.

We had a fucking symphony going with both our sons screeching, but it was music to my tired ears. Tears filled my eyes when she handed the second baby to me and the first one to Jake. This child was considerably larger than our first, but Kerry was satisfied they were both equally healthy. Further tests would take place at the hospital.

The placenta was birthed and both Jake and I were relieved when Kerry declared there would be no more surprises. Two babies were going to test my mothering skills, I hoped I was up to the challenge. I was certainly going to appreciate ma's help now.

Gonzo left the room and returned with a gurney. Jake lifted me on and a baby was placed into each of my arms before the sides were raised to keep us safely tucked in.

Maree and Sally hugged and kissed me, they both had tears in their eyes and mine filled too. Jake followed me out to the ambulance and before I was lifted in, he captured my lips in a loving kiss.

"I'll ask Maree to take care of things here and follow you in the truck." He brushed his lips over mine while Kerry and Gonzo waited patiently.

Once in the ambulance, I fell into a contented sleep.

Chapter Twenty-One

CALLIE

The nurse helped Jake strap our sons into their capsules in the back seat of his truck while I climbed into the passenger seat. I couldn't wait to get home and be in my man's arms. Jake slid into the driver's seat, leaned over and kissed me.

My man looked exhausted. "You look tired, sweetheart." I knew he'd been busy over the last three days and he'd spent hours at the hospital with me and our sons. The nurses had shown him how to bathe and diaper our babies and he insisted on doing it while I rested.

Maree, Mitch, and the girls had visited the previous day. It was the first time Rosy and Ella had seen the boys and they were excited. We sat them on the bed and they nursed one baby each, it was cute hearing them cooing to them in baby language. They were going to be the best cousins to our sons.

Maree had been staying at our place to help Jake out and said he'd been going non-stop getting the nursery ready for when we went home. We hadn't factored in needing two of everything.

"Maree and I have been busy, the nursery is ready for Allan and Mathew. What is it with you women, she wouldn't let me buy half of what I wanted either?"

"They don't need it Jake, babies grow fast and a lot of it wouldn't be used." I justified Maree's decision.

"I guess. Everyone is at the house to welcome you home, I told them one hour and then they have to leave. I mean, for fuck sake, they all came and saw you in the hospital and had a cuddle of the boys. Maree is ready to return home and she texted me to say she'd picked Ma and Dad up at the airport and they're settled into the guest room."

"They're just excited for us, sweetheart, and you promised to tell them the boy's names when I came home. I love you so much, thank you for everything."

Jake gathered my hand, lifted it to his lips and kissed it softly. At the speed he was driving, it would be an hour before we even reached home.

Oh, I better bring you up to date on the boys. Allan Bailey Prescott, our first born weighed in at 5lbs 1oz and 17 inches long. After numerous tests, he was declared healthy. Mathew Jake Prescott was our big boy, he weighed in at 8lbs 4ozs and measured 20 inches in length. He was also given a clean bill of health. We'd been assured it wouldn't take long for Allan to catch up to his brother.

When Jake pulled the truck into our garage, the butterflies started, I was terrified of meeting his parents. Jake rounded the truck and helped me down. I waited while he lifted Allan's capsule out and handed it to me. He was sound asleep, so precious. Jake lifted out Mathew who was fussing a little and we entered the house through a side door which opened into the kitchen.

We stepped inside to find a sea of faces smiling our way. The cheers and clapping were deafening and set both boys to bellowing in fright. Jake lifted his hand for silence but it was too late. I unstrapped Allan and lifted him onto my shoulder, Jake did the same for Mathew.

"Sorry," Viking Dave said sheepishly. His apology was echoed by the others.

"It's fine, sooner or later they'll have to get used to your loud voices."

Jake wasn't quite as generous, he was going to be overprotective I feared. "You need to learn to be quiet when my sons are around. You'll give them nightmares if you keep startling them."

A short, stout woman burst through the gathering and wrenched Allan from my arms.

"Stop fussing, son, a little noise never hurt anyone. Do you think the club members tiptoed around you and your sister?" She held out her free arm for Mathew and Jake placed him in it before kissing her cheek.

"Callie, meet Ma. She's a regular Sargent-Major but you'll get used to it."

I would have known who she was even if she hadn't called Jake, son, or I hadn't been introduced. She looked exactly like the photos of her scattered throughout the house. I stepped forward and stood nervously, unable to shake her hand because they were full of our children. "Pleased to meet you, Mrs. Prescott."

"It's Ma, now kiss my cheek." She gave me a warm smile and it set me at ease.

Then I heard a booming voice from behind everyone and Jake shrugged before mouthing *Dad*. He'd told me his dad was loud and there was no hope of keeping him quiet. "Where are my new grandsons? Fuck me if the boy didn't do his old man proud. Two princes to join my two princesses. I'm a happy man, where are they are?"

A giant of a man stepped forward. Fuck, he was at least a half head taller than Jake's six feet five inches. I had to stifle a giggle when he stood beside Jake's ma who was all of five feet nothing. My man had his arm wrapped around my waist and he held out the other to shake hands with his father.

"This must be my daughter-in-law, you did good kid." He leaned forward, wrapped his hands around my waist, lifted me into the air and placed a kiss on both cheeks.

"Dad, put my woman down."

Everyone laughed when he set me back on my feet and Jake pulled me possessively into his side.

"You got a looka, son. Now, where the fuck are my grandsons."

"Will you quiet down, Jake, you'll scare the crap out of them," Ma growled.

We watched as our sons were settled into the giant man's arms, they looked so tiny. He crossed the room and settled onto the sofa. Tears burned my eyes as I watched him softly cooing and kissing their foreheads.

"Okay, little brother, we want names. We've waited long enough."

I nodded and Jake spoke. "Tyler, Bailey, where are you?"

I was thrilled when they stepped forward arm in arm, Justin in Tyler's arms, Jane and Peter by their sides.

"Welcome home, Callie and congratulations on the safe birth of your sons." Bailey's sentiments were echoed by others in the room.

"Names," Maree said firmly. Her hands fisted on her hips.

"Our big man is Mathew Jake." My man turned toward his father. "Dad, the Jake is for you. We talked about it as his first name, but when you said you were moving back to be near your grandkids, we thought three Jakes in one place was a bit much."

Jake's dad nodded and when he lifted his face, tears shone in his eyes. "Thanks, son. Thanks, Callie."

I swiped at my tears.

"Love you, dad, don't think you're getting your club back though."

We all laughed.

"Don't want it, son. I might join you for the occasional ride but I want to spend time with these four." Ella and Rosy had climbed up on the sofa beside their Grandpa and were snuggled into him.

"Okay, now..." Jake fixed his eyes on Bailey. "Our little boy is Allan Bailey. Without you, Bailey, I wouldn't have my beautiful, bad woman back by my side and I wouldn't have known my sons. I owe you everything, man. You ever need anything, you pick up the phone and call."

Bailey nodded, tears flooded his cheeks. Tyler handed Justin to Jane, gathered his husband in his arms and held him tight.

A lump stuck in my throat and tears welled in my eyes. I stepped in front of Jake and buried my face in his chest. He folded me in his arms and kissed the top of my head.

Jake didn't allow the melancholy to last, and I found myself at the table, eating, drinking—nonalcoholic, even though I wasn't breast feeding I needed to be alert for our sons—and laughing while our babies were passed from one set of welcoming arms to another.

When the boys fussed for a feed, Jake called a halt to the festivities saying they were due to be fed and I needed to rest. I warmed up their bottles and Ma fed Allan while Dad fed Mathew, giving Jake and I the opportunity to see everyone out.

***

It had been six weeks since the babies came into the world and they've grown like weeds. Jake and I are exhausted but blissfully happy. His mother has been a life saver as Jake needed to go back to work two weeks after they were born. I have no idea how I would have coped without her. Jake misses his sons, but makes up for it when he comes home.

Ma and Dad head home tomorrow to organize the sale of their condo and to start packing. We've told them they are welcome to stay here until they have a place of their own. Maree was right, Ma has the balance perfect between being helpful and interfering. I'll miss them when they leave, not only their help, but the love and attention they also shower on me.

There was a soft knock and I called out to come in. Psycho swung the bedroom door open and I turned to look at him. He was wearing the same as Jake and his best man, Viking Dave. Black pants, white shirt, and red tie. His beard has been trimmed and his motorcycle boots—none of them would compromise on not wearing their boots and I didn't push it—are polished to a mirror shine. He certainly looked handsome.

He let out a soft whistle as he stepped forward and my face heated.

"Pres' eyes are gonna pop out of his head when he sees you. You'll have his dick at least at half-mast for the whole of the ceremony. I know where you'll be when you disappear."

Maree helped me buy the dress I was wearing. I wanted something sexy but feminine.

Like the wedding, I didn't want frills and flounces. The dress fell to my knees, hugging my curves on the way down. It was black lace with nude colored lining, the back dips to my waist, but the front has a high, round neckline. My glossy brown hair has been curled and tousled, left loose as Jake wanted. Makeup is natural with a smear of peach colored lipstick. The black, strappy sandals on my feet make my long legs seem even longer. I feel like a princess. Jake's princess.

I laughed as I put the finishing touches to my hair. The men are crude spoken but soft hearted. To see them with our sons, you'd never guess some of them were hardened ex-cons. They're good men now thanks to Jake's guidance and his father before him.

Psycho was thrilled when I asked him to walk me along the red carpet to where my man would be waiting for me. I have developed a close relationship with Psycho, he comes to the house and we work on the books while the boys are sleeping. He's old enough to be my father and treats me like a daughter.

He offered his arm and I slipped my hand around his elbow. When we reached the back door leading out to the garden, we find Maree and the girls waiting. She's wearing a knee length pink lace dress, not quite as figure hugging as mine. Rosy and Ella are dressed in white and full of excitement as they wait with their baskets of rose petals. Maree handed me one of the white rose bouquets she was holding and kissed my cheek.

"My brother won't know what hit him when he sees you. You look absolutely gorgeous."

The music began—*I Can't Help Falling In Love* by *Elvis Presley*, my favorite song. The girls walked side by side throwing rose petals over the carpet and some of the guests. They were so damn cute. Maree followed behind while Psycho and I watched from the side of the doorway. When she reached Jake, Viking Dave, and the Celebrant, she turned and everyone stood up from the white chairs where they'd been sitting.

"Time to get hitched, kid." Psycho kissed my cheek and led me into the doorway where we paused for a moment

I heard gasps, oohing and aahing, but it was Jake's gorgeous chocolate eyes I was locked on as we descended the steps to the strip of red carpet. He smiled, his eyes full of love as we made our way toward him.

Psycho handed me over to Jake, and again kissed my cheek before he was seated beside Ma and Dad who were holding our sleeping children. They offered to take care of them tonight so Jake and I can have some time alone at a hotel in Corgette. We hadn't been able to fuck since we'd been back together although, I had taken matters in hand to ensure Jake had relief. He's so horny all the time and said it's my fault for being so damn beautiful.

I have the all clear from the doctor now and I can't wait for us to be alone. Jake said he wanted our wedding night to be extra special, and since the boys had arrived, we decided to wait the six weeks, to get the all clear before marrying. A wedding night without love wouldn't have been the same.

Jake leaned over and whispered, "you're so gonna get fucked tonight. You look fucking gorgeous."

I giggled and glanced down to see Psycho was right, his cock was at half-mast.

The celebrant cleared her throat and with ours hands squeezed tightly together, we turned to face her.

The vows passed in a blur and we managed to say all the right words in all the right places. When Jake was told he could now kiss the bride, he swept me into his arms and gave me a spine-tingling kiss. His hard cock pressed into my belly. I knew I was in for a wild ride once we were alone. When he stood me back on my feet, he turned me slightly and groaned.

"What?"

"Fuck, no back and the swell of your ass is sexy as fuck."

I giggled as we turned to face our family and friends who clapped, cheered, and whistled. Our sons were both screaming, but as unfazed as ever, Ma and Dad stood and carried them up to the quiet of the house. Jake and I would be getting a night full of cuddles before we left for the hotel. I didn't know who would miss them the most, me or my husband.

"Happy, Mrs. Prescott?"

"You have no idea how happy, Mr. Prescott."

We stepped forward and I was engulfed in hugs, kisses, and gushed over. My heart soared.

I was surrounded by family and friends I loved and adored as they do me.

I have a husband who I love with every cell in my body.

I have two gorgeous sons who I'm besotted with.

The man by my side, the people before me, have pieced me back together and I know I'll never be bad again.

THE END

About the Author

Susan Horsnell writes romance from sweet to hot.

Strong social themes are a feature in her books.

She grew up in Manly, NSW, Australia, and has traveled Australia and the World on postings with her Naval Officer husband of 48 years.

She lives with her husband and fur baby – Gemma-Jean, a young Jack Russell Terrier, in a small village in the mountains in Queensland, Australia.

Since retiring from a nursing career of 37 years, she has been able to indulge her passion for writing.

The family enjoys traveling the country with their RV when not at home renovating.

Author Links

Newsletter:
http://eepurl.com/hyPb5L

SUSAN HORSNELL
Linktree
https://linktr.ee/SusanHorsnell

SUSAN R. HORSNELL
Linktree:
https://linktr.ee/SusanRHorsnell

Milton Keynes UK
Ingram Content Group UK Ltd.
UKHW021837031123
431812UK00015B/501